APACHE JACK

NATIVE VISIONS & STORIES

BY JACK RANDOM

CROW DOG PRESS
TURLOCK CA USA

Apache Jack:

Native Visions & Stories

By Jack Random

Published by
Crow Dog Press
1241 Windsor Court
Turlock CA 95380

Cover art by Ray Miller. Cover Photos by Camillus S. Fly, Sierra Madres, March 1886.

ISBN-13: 978-0997788303
ISBN-10: 0997788305

APACHE JACK

NATIVE VISIONS & STORIES

BY

JACK RANDOM

FORWARD

As a writer and a human being, Jack Random is an enigma. He personifies the duality of man. His bloodline runs through Oklahoma, aka Indian Territory, where the Trail of Tears once ended, where the European invaders crossed paths and intermarried with the Apache, Cherokee, Arapaho, Chickasaw, Blackfoot and Lakota. The offspring of an Idaho sharecropper and a California pugilist, he has at times felt equally at home sitting around a fire circle or a poker table, in a sweat lodge or jazz joint, in the heart of a bustling city or in the isolation of a great southwest desert. He is a quiet man with a restless spirit. He is a spiritual man whose religious beliefs are grounded in mother earth.

Jack Random is many things and yet he is none of these. He is a writer and therefore he is what he writes. In the end it may be that we can never truly know another human being. We know what we gather through the senses. We know the observable, the persona or the exterior of an individual. What we know of an individual's soul we can only deduce. We know the mythology of a man. We get no more than a glimpse of the great mystery that is every man and every woman. Jack Random is a writer. He is what he writes. Nothing more. Nothing less.

In the summer of 1993 the writer received word that his great grandmother on his father's side, Mary Noriega, who had been thought of Hispanic origin, was in fact a full-blood Apache. While other family members subsequently disputed that report, it affirmed a deep empathy for the native peoples of this continent and led to a series of writings featuring native beliefs, culture and characters.

The stories in this collection date back to 1996 when *Desert Dreams* was published as a handbook. Sent to the Pine Ridge reservation it somehow found its way to Long Standing Bear Chief of the Blackfoot tribe in Montana. He expressed concern that so many of the stories involve alcohol abuse and self-pity. "Let's get beyond the anger of mourning." In response to the story Ghost Dance, he wrote: "This is a story of revenge. It scares me. Is there another way for us to get justice? I think so. Bring the whites to our way of belief and prayer." I did not fully appreciate his comments then. I do now.

Apache Pilgrim was first published in 1997 (Crow Dog Press). Ghost Dance was originally published in *Liquid Ohio* and The Killing Spirit in *Haight Ashbury Literary Journal*.

TABLE OF CONTENTS

ILLUSTRATIONS

DESERT DREAMS

Land of the Coyote

APACHE JACK

The first time I met Apache Jack I was in a bar in southwest New Mexico. So was he. Drinking mescal like it was tumbleweed juice, sitting in a circle of wild-eyed Mescalero Apache, he told me he was studying with a spirit guide – what the white man calls a medicine man – and invited me to attend a ceremony. I did not know at that time the nature of the strange seed I ingested that night in an atmosphere of silent and solemn reverence.

The medicine man appeared ancient, the lines of his face like canyons and crevices, a map of the earth that shaped him. I saw the lines of his ancestry, countless faces, all wise and deep in meditation, all bearing smiles of secret knowledge. He seemed illuminated with translucent green and gold like the desert around us. He spoke in tongues familiar yet indecipherable.

Jack radiated in white light, reverberating in shades of blue, changing to green and back again, fluctuating like some mystical lamp of the Orient.

The spirit guide smiled and nodded approval. The others bore light but it seemed weaker and tinged with a dark and reddish hue. They saw the attention the spirit guide paid this strange mestizo and jealousy marked their faces. They envied his immunity to their spells and charms. They envied the way he lived completely in the moment, unencumbered by the ghosts of his past, unchained to ambition and desire.

They envied the man and so did I.

I followed him into the desert where we walked the path of the coyote and slithered with the diamondback. He lifted me on his shoulders and we soared on the wings of a hawk through cloudless skies under a golden red moon. I gazed into the eyes of the crow, saw the future unfold in an instant and became lost in its spell. I awakened squinting into sunlight on a high desert mesa.

Gone. Alone. My eyes ached with wonder. I walked back to the pueblo and asked the medicine man where my friend had gone.

"He is here," he explained with that knowing smile. He placed his hand on his chest and extended it over the horizon.

It would be years before our paths would cross again but I would never learned more than I had that day. He would always be an enigma and a mystery.

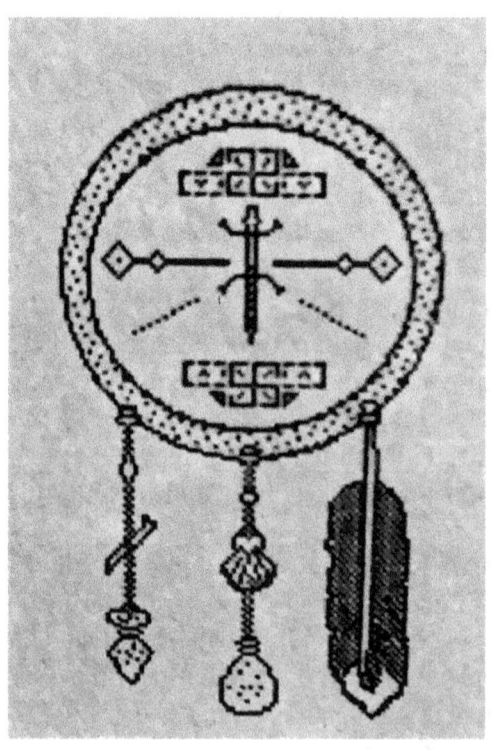

MITAKUYE OYASIN

Two legs, four legs, six legs, eight legs
All my relations

The cold wind of the north
The warm wind of the east
The harsh wind of the west
The gentle breeze of the south
All my relations

Herbs, flowers, plants and trees
All my relations

Those that walk the path
Those that walked before us
Those that will come
All my relations

The Great Peacemaker, the Christ Child,
Little Buddha and White Buffalo Woman
All my relations

Earth, air, fire and water
All my relations

Autumn, summer, winter, spring
The Great Wheel, the Seven Chakras and
The Tree of Knowledge
The sun, the moon, the planets and stars

JACK RANDOM

All my relations

French, Irish, British and Scottish
Choctaw, Apache, Cherokee and Sioux
Algonquin, Seminole, Montauk and Hoh
American, European, Asian and African
Forest, desert, mountains and coast
All my relations

Coyote, wolf, fox and bear
Whale, dolphin, salmon and shark
Eagle, hummingbird, swan and hawk
Beaver, horse, deer and buffalo
Snake, lizard, turtle and frog
Raven, crow, owl and bat
Butterfly, dragonfly, ant and spider
All my relations

I am the dreamer and I am the dream
I am the essence in all that I see
The earth and I are one
From the highest mountain to the depth of the sea
From the first of the species to the last
All beings and all things
All my relations

My tribe, my kin, my breath, my spirit
My glory and my defeat
My humility and pride
My sorrow and pain
The wonder and the love
All my relations

Mitakuye Oyasin

GERONIMO'S EYES

"I was with Geronimo," Jack said with a straight face. In the depth of his dark eyes you could see Geronimo's fire. You could dance with Apache warriors. You could see yourself reflected in Geronimo's eyes.

"I was a turncoat," he related without a trace of shame. "I joined the Wasichu army and tracked Geronimo down for the third and last time. I was on the train that took us all to prison in the Florida swamps. Only the swamps could contain a spirit as large as Geronimo's."

He took a slug of mescal and let the worm swirl in his mouth as his eyes rolled in his brain before he continued.

"I was on the train that took us all back to the Indian Nation in Oklahoma. I was in the passenger seat when Geronimo drove his Cadillac."

On the last syllable of his last spoken word he rose and howled like a blind wolf before he collapsed on the floor with a smile plastered to his face. He never spoke of Geronimo again.

Geronimo
Photo by De Lancey Gill circa 1905

COYOTE

He gained the confidence of a Chiricahua spirit guide who shared his vision as a father would his son. "To become the coyote you must see through the eyes of the coyote. You must breathe with the lungs of the coyote. You must run with the legs of the coyote. You must sniff the air with the scent of the coyote. You must think with the brain of the coyote. You must desire the meat of the rabbit as the coyote does."

To the untrained eye this land was empty and devoid of life but the old man saw beyond the silence. The desert exploded with life beneath the surface.

"If you do all this you will be as the coyote is but you will not be the coyote for you have the spirit of a man. To become the coyote you must bid farewell to the ways of a man, the thoughts of a man, the voice of a man, the conscience of a man. If you do all this you may not return to being a man but you will become the coyote."

Slowly Jack's vision became clear, clearer than it had ever been as a man. He saw the desert landscape, silhouetted in moonlight, from the level of the ubiquitous sagebrush. He let the sage scrape against his body as he passed, picking up its poignant scent, disguising the animal smell that he recognized as his own. He became aware of circling outward as if trying to distance himself from some unseen predator. Outward and outward, swiftly and silently, he moved with a grace he'd never known existed in the world of physical being. At length he slowed and raised his head to gage the wind. A sense of satisfaction enveloped him like a rush of warm blood centered in his loins and felt the muscles of his jaw curl into a smile. He became aware of his target, the focal point of his consciousness, more sentient than mental, more smell than vision. It was not a predator. He was the predator. He had spotted a herd of rabbits and zeroed in on the one that was slower than his fellows. A slight sprain or injury gave him a subtle hitch of movement and marked him for dinner.

The rabbit was in many ways more gifted than his species: Keener senses of smell and hearing, quicker and faster with greater endurance. But the rabbit's gifts were physical. His was the smarter and cleverer of species. The rabbits no doubt sensed his presence only minutes before but his circling led them to forget the danger. He had circled until the wind became his cover and his ally.

He rested a little longer to gather his strength and allow the illusion of safety to take hold. Now he closed in for the kill, slowly and secretly at first, allowing the herd to react before he broke into a sprint.

The lead rabbit sniffed the air and pointed his ears, the sign he had awaited. He quickened his pace and as the herd broke for cover he zeroed in on the lesser one. The chase ended almost before it started. He grasped the rabbit's neck in his jaws and shook until he felt its strength collapse, its breath extinguish. Only then did he become aware of a rush of power and energy that dominated his whole being. This was the kill. It was a magical feeling of wonder and intense excitement. He relished it as he felt it slowly subside as he carried his still writhing prey to a place in the rocks sheltered from wind and sight. There he devoured it, ripping at its throat so that its struggle ceased, tearing its flesh from bone, leaving little on its skeletal remains.

Profoundly satisfied, he climbed to a high point on the rocks and let loose a victory cry. He had solved the nightly problem of hunger and now he felt mischievous. He sniffed the air and sensed at once the presence of his lone predator.

APACHE JACK

A curious smile returned to his jaw muscles. There were times when he would flee – when he was weak or hungry or when his scent spoke to him of eminent danger. Not this time. This was a man who was at home in the desert. This was a man who remained still in the desert moonlight. This was a man worth experiencing. This time he would play. He found his most comfortable pace and closed the distance until the man came into sight. He stopped momentarily and began to circle, searching for a place to observe this strange human without being observed. He settled on a rock shrouded by sage, slowed his breath to silence and watched.

The man appeared as humans generally appear in the desert but his manner was different. He sat motionless and upright on his own rock, open to the world as if he had no fear and wished to be observed by the creatures of the desert night. The remains of a fire smoldered before him, its coals still glowing with warmth. He had observed his prints when circling: they were smooth and soft on the earth. He belonged to a particular breed of men who knew and valued the way of the land. In some ways he was more dangerous than others of his species but less threatening, less disturbing. He would leave little of himself behind.

He watched for what seemed a long time, perceiving no movement, when a curious idea came into his head and gave him great joy. He would leave his mark on the man. Slowly he emerged from his hiding place and moved to where the man sat breathing in the slow, tempered and melodic pattern of sleep. His eyes remained closed, his forearms outward, resting on his folded legs, enchanted by the moon.

He paused, poised to dash for cover, but relaxed when the man did not stir. He could observe no movement and no sign of awareness. He inched forward until he was no more than a rabbit's leap away, paused again, and again inched forward. His jaws curled into the smile of a lifetime as he raised his hind leg and relieved himself on this being.

19

Drained, he backed away to observe his marking and started when he saw that the man's eyes were open and trained to his. Still the man did not move. He stopped and stood still. They stared into each other's eyes, each seeing infinitely more than could be absorbed or understood. The man saw the eyes of the coyote. The coyote saw the eyes of the man. They each saw through each other's eyes and became enrapt until they smiled at the same precise instant.

The coyote went his way.

Jack was back.

DESERT RATS

The old cowpoke in mother-of-pearl snap button shirt, weathered hat and plain brown cowboy boots stared at him with the bitterness of a generation of cowboy hero movies.

"Round 'em up, boys," he heard him thinking. "We got us an Injun to take care of."

It was the moccasins that gave him away. Apache moccasins had upturned toes made for long-distance running. Geronimo's children were quick on their feet. They could cover five hundred miles of desert in a day. They could move mountains and dance on clouds and the old cowpoke was scared to death of them.

"What's the matter, boy?"

He downed the last of his whiskey to provide the courage his spirit lacked. His hand trembled before he landed it on the bar.

"The government didn't give y'all enough land you got to come to ar'n?"

Jack could only assume that "ar'n" meant ours. He was well versed in the English language but these desert rats had their own version that was sometimes hard to unravel. It was easy to see this wasn't the first time the old cowpoke had spun this particular yarn.

"Oh, I fergot! They don't sell al-kee-hal on the reserve!"

Jack didn't bother to explain that he didn't live on the reservation. It didn't matter. He raised his right hand, palm outward, and said: How! It was the Indian way of covering every possible inquiry or response: How's the farm? How's the road? How's it been? How's it going? The white man never said what it was and the Indian never asked. "How" was actually the Oglala incantation for "It is good" or "Let it be so" much as the Christian imparts "Amen!"

But "how" seemed to do the trick. The old cowpoke laughed and bought him a drink. They didn't engage in conversation. They preserved the illusion that they did not share the same language. The illusion was more honest than the truth. A language is more than words. It is the sharing of signs, symbols, values and mythology. It is the spirit of a human being and a culture. They did not share the same language but they each realized there was a way of accepting and acknowledging the other's place in the world.

Jack smiled like a television Indian and bought the next round. "How!" he thought. How!

KACHINA

"Everything that exists in the mind of man exists in the physical world," he said between doses of chewing tobacco and shots of corn whiskey.

The old man was decidedly crazy and Jack wondered why he took him seriously.

"How can that be? Do we create the nightmare with our thoughts? Do we dream up our own ghosts? Do we invent our own monsters? Are we stalked and haunted by our own darkness? Is that how it works?"

"Idiot!" the old man barked, hoisting another shot, its yellow residue dribbling down the cracks of his cheeks. Jack waited but the old man just stared him down with contempt.

"Then how, old man?"

"I'll tell you how."

He wiped the dribble across his chin and tried for a moment to recover some semblance of his sane and sober self.

"Memory," he said finally, as if no other explanation was necessary or forthcoming.

"Memory?" Jack inquired. He was suddenly dedicated to seeing this one through. He wanted to know the old man's theory. Suddenly nothing else mattered. Only this.

"We humans are such fools," the old man said, aware of the change in his young drinking partner's level of interest. "We think we can control everything. We think we create! We create nothing! We control only what we perceive."

Jack began to understand.

"If we believe in spirits, they appear before our eyes. If

we believe in ghosts, monsters, vampires or alien beings, there they are. If we don't believe we see nothing. Not because they aren't there. They're there all right. You can bet on that! You can take it to the bank! We just don't see them. That's how it is, my young friend. That's how it's always been."

With that he passed out face first on the bar. Jack smiled and shook his head. At last he understood. He knew instinctively the old man was right. He put a five spot in the old man's pocket and bought him a bottle before he walked out into the desert air. He breathed deep and gazed up at a sky of a million stars.

A cylindrical object with a green and golden glow darted toward him, hovered and vanished, leaving only a trace of translucent light across the desert sky. He tipped his hat and hit the road.

OYAH HO HOYAH

Chant of the Owl

Oyah ho hoyay, Oyah ho hoyah...

O Great Spirit hear my prayer
I ask not for wealth
I ask not for freedom
I have no want of food or shelter
But O Great Spirit let me be wise

Oyah ho hoyay, Oyah ho hoyah...

O Great Spirit hear my cry
I am lost within my land
I am lost within my home
I am lost within my self
I have love and many comforts
But O Great Spirit let me be wise

Oyah ho hoyay, Oyah ho hoyah...

O Great Spirit hear my plea
I listen to the wind
I look for the signs
I plant my feet upon the earth
But O Great Spirit let me be wise

JACK RANDOM

Oyah ho hoyay, Oyah ho hoyah...

O Great Spirit hear my song
I offer you the breath I breathe
I offer you my soul
I offer you the sacred seed
O Great Spirit let me be wise

Oyah ho hoyay, Oyah ho hoyah...

SAND CREEK

Driving across the desert skyline of southern Colorado in an old Chevy pickup, flat base gray and slowly rusting, Jack felt himself being pulled by an external force. The sight of a raven on a telephone line drew his vision toward the glare of the sun and in that instant he found himself spinning, fishtailing out of control, off the pavement of the two-lane highway, kicking up a great cloud of dust, dirt and sand.

When he came to rest the world was no longer upright. He was not hurt. He had no difficulty climbing out of his truck. He had no concern for his state of mind or the health of his vehicle. The unseen spirit of the land pulled him forward, commanding all of his attention. He had seen this spirit before and knew the futility of fighting back.

He walked into the sandy desert, across the barren sagebrush land, to a distant oasis of dogwood and willows. He heard spirit voices crying in anguish and desperation. He saw many tipis and through the smoke and dust he made out the figure of an old man raising a white flag beneath the red, white and blue of the Wasichu nation. The voices grew louder and the cries more desperate. He saw soldiers in blue uniforms and heard the volleys of their gunfire. He felt the reverberation of their cannon. He saw women and children running to the creek nearby as the men scrambled for their weapons. He saw bluecoats tearing the clothing from native women, slicing scalps and mutilating the bodies of children in an orgy of blood and slaughter. He watched the old man's eyes turn from cold disbelief to a raging fire of hatred. He stood his ground as the gunfire ripped at tipis all around him until at length he joined his people in retreat.

A bullet pierced Jack's heart and he collapsed to the ground in horror, grasping the earth with both hands, tears swelling in his eyes, blood streaming from the hole in his chest.

An old codger placed his hand gently on Jack's shoulder and looked into his aching eyes.

"You alright? I seen your truck back there by the road and followed your trail out here."

Jack rose to view the aftermath of slaughter, death and destruction. Bodies lay everywhere and everywhere their blood settled into the earth. Finally he made out the old man's face and saw at once he was not of this time and place. He had kind and gentle eyes. He was not a killer of women and children.

"You alright?" the old man repeated, helping Jack to his feet.

"What is this place?" he asked.

The old man looked around as if hunting for signs.

"Goes by the name of Sand Creek."

"Sand Creek?" Jack repeated.

"Yes sir, they say there was a big Injun battle here a hundred year ago. They got one of them historical markers down by the roadside."

They walked back to the road where a tow truck was already tending to his pickup. They towed his truck to the nearest town but Jack declined the ride. He remained at this sacred site for seven days, living on rabbits, snakes and berries. He built a sweat lodge, held a ceremony for his fallen ancestors and left his own historical marker carved in stone: Here was the Sand Creek Massacre, 1864.

GHOST DANCE

He did not see what was directly before him because his mind, his spirit, the soul of his being, his undiscovered self, had been transported elsewhere. He was himself yet he was not himself. He was his dream self. He was dreaming yet he was aware of dreaming. He could control his movements, direct his vision and his thoughts. Standing beside him was a spirit guide with deep probing eyes. He did not say he was a spirit guide but Jack knew, just as he knew this man was his ally and his friend.

"I am Song of the Wind," he said. He spoke in his native tongue yet Jack understood his words. He gestured to a circle of chanting Lakota Indians.

"Here the People dance. They dance the dance of the Ancestors. It is the dance that makes the earth tremble and signals the coming of floods, winds and pestilence. They sing that the spirit of the old ones not be forgotten. They pray that the lost take their places upon the earth once more, that the great mother remember those who are her friends and that she punish those who are her enemies."

He looked deep into Jack's eyes.

"It is the dance the white eyes call the Ghost Dance. It is the dance of Big Foot and Black Elk, Crazy Horse and Sitting Bull, Kicking Bear and High Hawk. It is the dance of the Paiute and Shoshone, Cherokee and Cheyenne, Kiowa and Crow, Apache and Arapaho, Navaho and Comanche. It is the dance of the Hunkpapa and Minneconjou at Wounded Knee."

The old man's piercing gaze was relentless as he reached

into Jack's soul.

"I have thought long before allowing you to see this but there is no other way. I have decided that an Indian is here." He pressed his leathered hand to his chest. "I have decided that you are one with the People."

Jack pressed both hands in fists to his chest and extended them outward. It meant: I am honored and I give myself to your hands.

The circle of dancers opened to them. They linked arms with the others and began to move in perfect harmony with the whole of the sacred circle. When it came time for him to sing the words came to him without thought. They sang of a time that was past, a time that is present and a time that would come. They wore the sacred robes that shielded them from the white man's bullets. They danced and sang for hours and hours until time ceased to function. There was only movement and sound and spirit. There was only emotion and reverence and joy in being.

A large man whose countenance identified him as a great chief broke off from the circle and moved to the center, his open palms to the heavens, his eyes shining with the fire of ancient grief. The People began to chant to an ancient drumbeat:

We cannot be free we cannot be free…

The chief fell to his knees and spoke in a voice that shook the nearby mountains and reverberated in every particle of his being.

Until the rings of power are worn again by mother earth and father sky…

We cannot be free we cannot be free…

Until the Wasichu gods are fallen and the pale face masters die…

We cannot be free we cannot be free…

Howl of the wolf and the eagle's cry, caw of the crow and song of the wind, I have been to the sacred mountain, I have walked the plains of the buffalo, I have swimmed the stream

of the salmon, I have danced the song of the whistling pine, I have ridden the smoke of the ancient flame and talked with the tallest trees. I have heard the voice of our ancestors cry out: *We must be free!*
We cannot be free we cannot be free...
We must be free!
A great army of blue coats appeared on all sides. The chief rose and let loose a war cry that cracked the sky with thunderbolts and shook the ground: *Ai-yai-yai-yai-yai-yai!* The white men with their Hotchkiss guns warmed and loaded opened fire on the crazed Indians who continued their dance and pushed their chant to a crescendo. The chief leapt and scurried about on all fours, a wild and crazy dance of the coyote, yipping and howling at an unseen moon.

This time the faithful did not fall. This time their sacred shirts protected them as they danced and chanted and prayed. The sky opened like flood gates and pelted the offending army with a torrent of rain. The earth cracked and swallowed them whole while the Indians still danced and chanted and prayed. They danced into and out of the night. They danced until they collapsed the next day, when the sun shined more brilliantly than any of them could remember.

The ancestors laughed in silence at the universal smile that graced their native faces.

The Ghost Dance survives!

[A comment from Long Standing Bear Chief: This is a story of revenge. It scares me. Is there another way for us to get justice? I think so! Bring the whites to our way of belief and prayer!]

Ghost Dance
Photo by James Mooney circa 1891

PRAYER OF WHITE WOLF

"Great Spirit! We thank you for the offerings we have received this night. We thank you for the second sight."

He smoked and refilled the pipe for another pass around the circle. He sat Indian style but his hands were folded in the manner of a Zen master. He raised his eyes and palms skyward as he spoke.

"I am the wolf, the teacher and the hibernating bear. My friends are the lizard and the coyote. This night I have howled at the moon and received wisdom without words. I have sought the comfort of my kind and enjoyed the beauty of being alone with my inner being. Through the eyes of the crow I know the divine oneness of all creatures, no lesser nor greater than myself. For this and many things I cannot know I give thanks."

EYES OF THE CROW

Through the eyes of the crow
A barren landscape breathes translucent energy
Pulsating within its loins
Palpable and illuminating
The force of all being

Down through the sacred spiral
Down through the tunnel of mystery
Down through the void of all and nothing
Down through the eyes of the crow

Concealed in the shadows of the lizard king
A waking dream reveals all things
And pulls at the eyes of the crow

The wolf howls at the moon in full
A dragonfly on its perch
The hawk soars and the redbird sings
Coyote prowls its circular path
A brown bear stirs in its cave
Snake sheds its skin and goes
All through the eyes of the crow

All is one within the soul
As one is all without
Each creature has its appointed place
Looking through the eyes of the crow

THE VISION

Jack parked his truck at a lookout along the highway and went into the desert not knowing why or where his moccasins would take him. Carrying only a knife and a water pouch he walked toward a distant rock formation, which somehow captured the image of a fluttering, glowing crow, shimmering in the shadows of a dying sun. The crow was his totem animal. An elder of the Navaho tribe who called herself a child of the earth gave it to him. It was his helper, guide and protector.

He walked away from the sun and welcomed the cool blue light of an August moon. He watched the landscape change, the shadows growing longer until they were replaced by moon shadows in deeps shades of purple and gray. He walked through the night and into the day and the warmth of morning light soothed him, his eyes still fixed to the crow shaped mountain. He did not think of food or sleep. His mind as empty and distant as deep space, his body grew tired and hungry and weak.

He reached the shadow of Crow Mountain when he fell to the earth and a fever took hold of him.

A white buffalo appeared before him and he watched it transform to a beautiful maiden as told in Lakota lore.

"Wa-ya-ka, wa-oo-ya," she intoned, palms extending outward, inviting, comforting and calming. He gave his spirit to her, clutching the sand beneath him and rising to toss the sand in the four sacred directions. When he completed the circle, he walked with the maiden, mounting golden horses and riding to the heavens as she gestured to the sights that appeared below.

He saw the endless plains of buffalo, the ancient hunting grounds alive with deer, elk, moose, antelope and black bear. He saw streams of salmon, trout, beaver, kingfisher and the great blue heron. He ran with the coyote, swam with the seal and soared on the wings of the eagle, hawk, owl and dove. But it was the crow that became his guide to the spirit world. It was the crow who heard his thoughts and spoke to him as a grandfather to a young boy. It was the crow who led him to the mountaintop and lifted him through the sacred rings. And as he rose through cloud-like circles he understood what was revealed. It was not a journey through space but through time. It was not the past but the giving of the past to the future.

"This is the promise," the maiden said. "This is the world that should be."

As he glared with eyes of stone at the vision of her beauty, she was again transformed to a very old woman with deep lines of wisdom and a feeling of sadness.

"It is the time of the great transformation," she said. "The air must be cleansed, the water purified. The old must die for the young to thrive."

In clouds of smoke and dust he saw the bearded ones, the white eyes with their long rifles. He saw them kill the last buffalo. He saw the massacre of Wounded Knee. He saw the People encaged like the Wasichu's cattle. He saw towers of smoke and dead fish on the banks of poison rivers. He saw the great mushroom cloud of destruction, heard the cries of children, and witnessed the anguish of mothers and the rage of fathers. He saw the earth shake with anger and the coming of the great flood, the great freeze and the great drought. He saw plant life die and animals scatter in fear.

He saw the earth wiped clean and a new breed of humans walking the land in harmony with its fellow beings. He saw the red people revered for their knowledge of the old ways. He saw the Wasichu humbled by the sins of his past. He saw a new beginning, a rebirth of spirit, a transformation of the earth.

The old woman became the maiden and spoke with profound empathy.

"Go now and speak of these things to your people. The children of the earth must be prepared. Everything in nature is healing and harmony. Plants are the people's medicine. The air is the spirit. The water is the blood. Everything must be made pure. The poisons must be expelled. Go now and reveal the truth. Prepare them for the great change."

The crow resting on his left shoulder lifted and flew into the setting sun. Jack followed to his waiting truck. He left at once for Indian country. For as long as he would live he would speak of his vision to anyone who would listen.

For years he found many who heard his words but few who listened. For years he bore their derision and smiled. Until at last the prophecies unwound with dizzying speed. Then they listened. They listened as the world around them crumbled to dust.

"Too late," he would say with sorrow's eyes.

"Too little, too shallow, too late."

A GATHERING OF THE TRIBES

The tribes came together for a great feast, a festival of dance, music, gaming and story telling. The tales of the elders were paramount. Each evening as the sun gave way to fire light, the people gathered in fire circles to hear elders tell stories of their ancestry. Some bore the responsibility of committing the stories of their tribes to memory and would join the same circle night after night. Others roamed from circle to circle, gathering sacred knowledge and wisdom from the four corners of the earth.

Jack walked among them. Though he knew neither how nor why, he knew what they knew. He saw through their eyes. He breathed the air that fueled their collective soul and fused it to his own. He understood their language in all its tongues.

He listened to a circle of Navaho speak of the Spanish warriors with their suits of shining silver, suits that arrows cannot pierce. They spoke of fire sticks that coughed smoke and propelled small but heavy stones at great distances. They spoke of a spirit guide's vision that the invaders would come and come again and again like waves of the endless waters, each time in greater numbers than before.

A young Apache warrior held up the headpiece of a conquistador, an oddly shaped silver creation that resembled the crown of a Spanish cock. The circle laughed at the prophetic vision and raised a defiant cheer, secure in their belief that the Great Spirit would protect them. Jack did not laugh and neither did the elder sitting on a nearby log. He closed his eyes and remembered the past that revealed to him the future.

Three men and a woman sitting atop a sacred mound caught his attention just as he captured theirs. It was not a sense of familiarity that drew him to their circle. He did not know them. It was their dazed, almost ghost-like expression that pulled him in. It mirrored his own.

He stood immobile as if his spine had been severed at the neck. They did not belong here. He did not belong here. Like him they had traveled here from some distant point in time or space. To him, it was dream travel. Though he did not understand it except as it exists in the unknowable realm of the great mystery, he had experience the phenomenon in varied forms since childhood. He was always aware of the dream yet until this moment it seemed real and natural. He had been captured by the illusion of timelessness in a timeless reality. He believed.

But now he realized he was not alone among the visitors, the outsiders or the dreamers. Now the observer became the observed and with that realization the illusion came crashing down like the walls of an earthen fortress under siege. He felt naked and exposed.

He was drawn to them by an irresistible force, his body yielding before his mind could reflect. He climbed a ladder at the side of the mound and he realized that those who truly belonged were not aware of his presence. The visitors had only eyes and ears in this place. They could not act. They were spirits without physical bearing.

The other visitors greeted him with smiles of pure wonder. They were enchanted, their eyes glowing like dew in morning light. He joined their circle and smoked from a ceremonial pipe that they had lifted from the festivities.

"We didn't think they'd mind," said the tallest of the four, a sleek Cherokee with long black hair and a colorful headband. A woman with the round features of an Arapaho, hair braided to the small of her back, assured him they would return it. The others were Kiowa brothers who remained silent in their wonder. The Cherokee spoke:

"What we'd like to know is: Who followed who?"

He was stumped. He had wandered in his dream visions through time and space as if it was a birthright, never once considering that someone or some other entity might have paved the way. He assumed that others could travel as he had but until now he had never encountered a fellow traveler. He assumed it was his vision alone. Now it seemed possible that others could share the same vision.

"Did we follow you," the Arapaho woman asked, "or did you follow us?"

They spoke of time traces that they had used to visit the ancient Anasazi, the Natchez and the Mayan empire and always they had located the source of their journey or the source had found them. It was their purpose to trace the paths and chronicle the links of past, present and future. They believed he was the link.

Jack deferred and pointed to an elder spirit guide by a fire on the far side of the clearing. The four visitors stood at once and crossed the clearing to the old man's fire. Jack remained behind, bearing witness as the Cheyenne below him began a chant to the ancient spirits of their ancestors. He smiled at what seemed a great irony: They envisioned spirits of the past while spirits of the future gazed upon them.

He sprang to his feet and took a running dive from his perch atop the mound, soaring like a hawk and becoming the spirit of the crow. He landed gracefully in a cloud of dust and smoke in the center of the Cheyenne circle, joining them in their chant and dancing to the spirit of the crow. Their song and dance intensified until, hours later, Jack collapsed in exhaustion.

The last thing he remembered before slipping under was a sudden darkening of the sky and the wicked laugh of an unknown spirit, a laugh that only grew louder when it should have dissipated.

A strange and elder voice said:

"What is will always be, has always been, forever. Time is an illusion."

Crow Dog Shield

THE ENEMY

"You must be as the crow to see through the eyes of your enemy. You must feel his heartbeat and know his mind. When you have learned to walk in the land of visions, the land beyond this land of hands and legs, then the crow will guide you and you will see the face of your enemy. They are many faces but they are one.

"They are pale faces. Faces of the dead on living bodies. They are old beyond their years and gray with worry. They are cunning like the fox but not wise like the owl. Their bellies and their minds are filled but their hearts are empty. They have no passion for the earth or living things but their eyes yet burn with desire. It is not the want of things that feeds this fire. It is not the want of power.

"They collect things and power as the farmer gathers seed. It is not the thing itself but the fruit that will one day spring from it. The fire that burns within their souls is the desire to leave a mark upon the earth, to write their names in the great book for others to see when they are gone from this world. Without this, all that they have is nothing.

"These things I have seen and the vision I give to you for it will help you in your cause. These things I tell you for the cause of all living things upon the earth. You must always believe in the cause. In this you must never waver."

He smoked from the sacred pipe and closed his eyes as if receiving words from the spirit world. He passed the pipe to his young friend and student.

"When times seem dark help will come from unexpected sources. Always remember: Your friends are here." He placed his hand on his heart. "It is where your enemies cannot reach. Never doubt."

They spoke of many things: the earth, the heart, the cause, the song of the wind, the drum of the rain and desert flowers. They spoke of the crow and the power of dreams. They spoke of the coyote, the owl, the beaver and the bear. They spoke of space and time, the Great Spirit and the nature of being.

When their words no longer found voice, they sat in silence and listened to the sounds of the desert evening, the breath and pulse of the sacred earth. They listened and prayed for her eternal majesty.

They embraced and looked long into the other's eyes, where each revealed the spectrum of their life experience. Alas the old one broke the spell.

"I am Song of the Wind. That is the name my people have given me because I dream and speak of the harmony of all things. I will call you: Eyes of the Crow. I call you this because it is your gift to see what others may not see. From this time forward you and I are one and all that I have I lay at your feet. Go now and do not be afraid of your dreams. I go with you though I remain here."

Jack turned and began the long walk back to camp. He could not help but glance once over his shoulder. A coyote stood where the old man had been. Its yap sounded like laughter as it scampered to the east.

THE PROPHECY

Inspired by strange visions the elders of many tribes proclaimed the prophecy of the Ghost Dance had come to fruition. The Great Spirit blessed the Indian for his patience and perseverance. The sky over the ancient ruins of the Anasazi glowed in azure brilliance where the old one, elder of elders, sat and observed the world. He did not have to be told a new age was dawning in the land of the setting sun.

He closed his eyes and he saw the white man's rings of power tumble to the earth. The Ghost Dance had begun and the ancestors rejoiced.

He opened his eyes and a decade had passed. The whole of the land was now a sanctuary of native culture. He closed his eyes and became the crow, soaring over herds of buffalo and forests teeming with wildlife. He saw his people take hands with the white man, the brown, black and yellow, not as master to captive, not as conqueror to conquered, but as human beings of equal worth and value. He saw that all men and women, all beings of the earth had a place in the grace and glory of the Great Spirit. He saw all becoming one within and without, from the smallest to the greatest of mother earth's creatures.

The silent revolution came to pass. There was no account in the newspapers. There were no reports in the media and no reference in the history books. Yet an era of good will and prosperity had begun.

The old one saw that it was good and gave thanks. To all he gave his blessing.

"The Great Spirit has used us wisely," he thought.

APACHE JACK

A large black crow cawed, circled four times overhead and vanished without a trace.

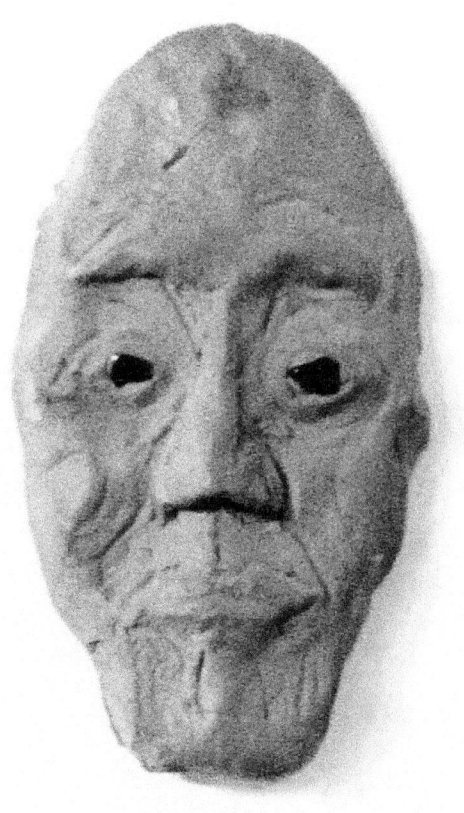

The Old One

APACHE PILGRIM

*To Our Great Grandmother
Mary Victoria Noriega*

INTRODUCTION

The mythology of the American west, even in the wake of recent revision, remains stronger than history. The word "Apache" conjures an image of fierce warriors murdering, scalping and butchering innocent settlers. While the Apache are not known for their spirituality they have a deeply spiritual cultural heritage. Like followers of Zen Buddhism they practice mindfulness in all activities. They believe in a universal cosmic force and the sacredness of all things.

Perhaps the best known of all Apache leaders, Geronimo was not only a fierce warrior, he was in fact a healer, a shaman and a vision seeker who strove to connect his people to the spirit world. Geronimo did not become the warrior we read about until the Spanish wiped out his family.

The participation of the Apache people in the Ghost Dance movement that affected virtually all plains Indians from the late 1880s to the turn of the century is little noted.

Apache Pilgrim is based on a historical anecdote from Charles Brant's *The Autobiography of a Kiowa Apache Indian* (Dover Publications 1969). The title story chronicles the pilgrimage of a young Apache to the home village of Wavoka, the seer who envisioned the Ghost Dance. The stories that follow are first person accounts of those he encounters along the way.

Central to this collection of stories is the need to bring the spiritual nature of the Apache people to light.

HISTORICAL BACKGROUND

By the year 1890 the heart and soul of the American West had undergone an irreversible transformation. The railroads had completed a transcontinental web only begun at Promontory Point in 1869, uniting north to south as well as east to west. Once thirty million strong and thriving, the buffalo had all but vanished.

Confined to reservations, Native Americans had survived a thirty-year policy of extermination. Having surrendered, Geronimo and his band of Chiricahua renegades had been banished to the swamps of Florida. The Oklahoma land rush had invaded Indian Territory and ranchers had parceled great expanses of the western plains, containing it in barbed wire.

Against this backdrop the greatest unifying movement in the history of Native America – greater even than the Confederacy of the Six Iroquois Nations – spread like a proverbial wildfire from Paiute country in northwest Nevada across the Great Plains until it reached the home of the Kiowa Apache in present day Oklahoma.

The tribe was filled with excitement and fear. They had heard a great deal of the prophet Wavoka's vision of the Ghost Dance. It was said that the ancestors would return to the world of the living. They had heard that the blue coats and their leaders feared the Ghost Dance so much that they prohibited all native peoples from dancing.

The Kiowa Apache sent a pilgrim to find Wavoka, speak to him and return to report what he had learned.

COYOTE EYES

I am Coyote Eyes of the Kiowa Apache. I am a healer, a man of the spirit world, seeker of visions, protector of the old ways and holder of sacred knowledge.

The spirit of the coyote gave me the power I possess. The coyote is a clever spirit, a trickster by nature. It took many years to understand his power and to control it. Since that time I have healed the sick, guided the blind and led the lost to the red road – the sacred path of our ancestors. I have brought people together in friendship who became enemies. I am a man of peace and good will.

I have had three visions in my life. The first came in the spring of the Wasichu year 1872. I went to the mountain where many had gone before me. It was my third visit, the third time I had fasted, prayed and deprived myself of sleep. I held my hand over the fire to stay awake. On the third day a vision came to me.

He appeared in the distance, across a deep ravine on a far peak. He watched me as I watched him. Despite the distance I could see his eyes and feel his presence bearing down on me, surrounding me, his spirit entering my body. My eyes grew weary. I blinked and he was gone. He appeared again to my left. When I turned he again vanished but I could hear his panting to my right.

"Coyote spirit, do not turn away," I pleaded. "I have come with open hands and heart, seeking guidance, wisdom and sacred power."

I turned to him and we gazed into each other's eyes. His were not the eyes of an ordinary coyote. They ran deep as the waters of a great lake and he spoke to me with these words:

You seek a vision and you will have one. In the camp where you lay your blanket a child is born with a crooked leg. Your people will fear him and believe he is touched by evil spirits. It is for you to set them right for this child has the gift of healing. It is not the sickness of the body he will heal but the sickness of the soul. He holds the medicine your people most need. Teach him and protect him. Do not fail him and the spirit will not fail you.

There are many things I wished to ask this spirit but the coyote is swift and illusive. I blinked again and he was gone. It would be many moons before I saw him again. By then the child with the crooked leg had grown into a fine young man, respected for his kindness and sound mind. I knew he would become what the coyote spirit foretold: a healer of the soul.

The world of the Kiowa Apache and all native peoples has changed. We have lost our freedom and our way of life. We have lost many of our best young men and women. We are lost as a people. We do not know what will become of us or even if we will survive.

The coyote spirit came to me again. This time I did not seek a vision. I sat with my brothers and sisters in a fire circle. He came to me in the flames. He said three great men of the northern plains tribes would come to our camp. They would bring word of an Indian prophet. He said we should listen to their words but hold back our heart and minds. He told me we should send a pilgrim to visit the prophet at his home. He said the young man with the crooked leg whom we named Walks Slowly should be chosen to this great task.

I thanked the coyote spirit and told the others what I had seen and heard. When three great men came and spoke to us of the Paiute Wavoka and the Ghost Dance, we honored the coyote's advice. We wanted to join them in the dance that promised to return our ancestors and free the people to live in the old ways. But we held back as the spirit wished.

APACHE JACK

We told Walks Slowly that he was chosen to take this sacred journey to the camp of Wavoka where the mountains touch the western sky. We plotted his route and told him all we knew about the land and the people he would meet. We asked him to visit our Apache brothers in New Mexico and Arizona and ask them about the Ghost Dance.

We gave him a good horse, a sacred pipe to give to the prophet, and many medicines and provisions. We also gave him a name that suited his status. From that time forward he would be known as Black Crow.

In the summer of the Wasichu year 1890 we received word from the north that the blue coats declared war on the Ghost Dance and murdered hundreds of Lakota at a place called Wounded Knee. When Black Crow did not return we feared the worst.

The coyote spirit came to me once more and told me Black Crow was alive and would return in the spring. He told me to continue my teachings and pass my sacred knowledge on to him. When the end of my trail arrived, I would tell him his pilgrimage was not over. He would journey once more.

I am proud of Black Crow. For though the Ghost Dance would not rise from the ashes of Wounded Knee, he would give the people hope. He would show us how to keep the ancestors alive within our hearts.

"The time will come," he said, "when we can do as we believe in our hearts. This is he war we can win. We must not forget. For all long as we remember the ancestors are with us and with us they will rise to live again."

HORSE THIEVES ON THE PECOS

Faraday's the name. William Faraday. Some folks call me Will, some call me Bill, and some whose mama's never taught them better call me names I'm not likely to repeat in mixed company. I can spin a by-golly-gee-wiz-you-don't-say yarn with the best of them. I've done all that Bill Cody did and then some. I've hunted buffalo, trapped and traded, scouted for soldiers, panned for gold, dug for silver, led a ragtag wagon train, fought Comanche, Sioux, Cheyenne and Apache. I've played poker and yanked the tiger's tail with the Earp boys, Doc Holliday and Wild Bill Hickok. I've rubbed elbows and then some with the Daltons, the Clantons and the Kid. I've smoked with the great Sitting Bull and parlayed with the one Injun everyone fears: Geronimo.

Along the winding path of my travels in the Wild West I've crossed paths with Kit Carson, Colonel Custer (never liked the man), Chief Joseph and Teddy Roosevelt – who had some fool notion he could shoot the last buffalo.

But of all my adventures, the one I look back on with the deepest affection is a stretch of trail I shared across Texas and Mexico with a young Kiowa Apache pilgrim. Wouldn't be right to call him a boy. He was a man and that he proved many a time but he had the face of a boy, soft and innocent. Couldn't have been more than seventeen, eighteen years old. He had a clubfoot. In all my days I never seen an Injun with such a deformity.

His white name was Abram Lincoln. Funny thing about them Oklahoma Injun agents: they liked to give Injuns the names of presidents. I've met four or five Ulysses Grants, Tom Jeffersons, George Washingtons and at least that many Abram Lincolns. He never told me his Apache name. They rarely did. Liked to keep it to their own. So of course I called him Abram.

He was on his way to Paiute country out Nevada way. Seems his people in Oklahoma took up the Ghost Dance and sent him to see its founder, a medicine man by the name of Jack Wilson – Injun name of Wavoka. I myself heard that Mr. Wilson was nothing but a lowdown shyster, a false prophet of the worst kind. I never shared that view with Abe. Figured it was up to him to decide.

We hooked up on the Red River and headed south by southwest – not the most direct route to Paiute country but his path would take him through the heart of Apacheria, the sacred Chiricahua Mountains, haunting grounds of Geronimo and Cochise. Even though there was no more than a handful of free Apaches left and those who were on the reservations were among the sorriest creatures on God's green earth, all that was up to Abram to figure out.

We headed out across the Texas plains to the Rio Grande, across the Grande to the Pecos, across the Pecos to the Mexican border and up north to New Mexico. A lot happens along the trail but mostly it happens inside. You ride with a man, pretty soon you come to know him. I can honestly say I not only liked Abram but I came to trust him like a brother.

Camped out on the Pecos we came across a situation that put us both to the test. Abram being young I couldn't be sure how he would react under the gun but I would soon find out.

It was late at night with only a sliver of moonlight in the Texas sky. There's a full trainload of riffraff, border trash and desperados around those parts so we took turns sleeping while the other kept a lookout. I was on watch and I recall thinking: Mighty quiet tonight. Too quiet. I was just about to doze off when I caught a whiff of something foul and odorous like the recollection of a woman scorned.

I woke Abram up and we took our positions hiding in the brush on both sides of the camp. Sure enough nine or ten of the foulest, most fiendish, ugliest, stinkiest, most miserable bunch of thieving, murdering desperados came riding up itching for blood. They was four Mexicans, four scraggly looking white men and one Injun – Jicarilla Apache I believe he was and Abram was right sorry to see it. They was trailing a string of seven horses so we knew good and well what they was about.

We were content to sit back and watch a spell as they went about their business cussing, spitting, hollering and drinking some vile Mexican whiskey, when the head honcho – an ugly fiend with a voodoo eye and a deep scar running the full length of his left cheek – took a stab at our coffee. That was all I was prepared to take. I shot the sombrero clean off his head, no doubt giving his scalp a good grazing. About that time Abram set to hooting and hollering one of them Apache war cries. I swear it sounded like three or four brave warriors and it got their attention.

I stayed well back and under cover and gave them a stern warning: "The name's Faraday! I've kilt more and better than the likes of you! So drop them guns or by God we'll drop you where you stand!"

Seemed they was just about to take me up on my offer when the honcho got an itch. Guess he figured he'd just as soon take his chances in a gunfight as to feel the burn of a hangman's noose. So I planted one betwixt his hideous eyebrows and all hell broke loose. Guns ablaze, bullets flying every which way, grown men screaming holy terror, hopping around like chickens with their heads chopped off.

I took down two more and Abram got two of his own as they was fixing to make their getaway. That was something we could not allow. Men like these get it in their craws that someone got the better of them, sure as dogs to a bone they'll come back looking to settle the score. We saw to it that weren't in the cards. Not this time, boys.

When the smoke cleared there was four of them left standing with their hands held high – one Mexican, two whites and one Apache – and praying for mercy. We hogtied them, set their horses free, put the dead afloat on the Pecos and captured a few precious hours of restless shuteye.

In the morning Abram said a few words for the departed to the Great Spirit and took up conversation with the hogtied Apache. He told Abram he'd been held captive. Said he had nothing to do with their thieving and killing. They got him drunk and used him as a scout to locate hideouts and getaway trails in Apacheria.

To my way of thinking it was a tossup. A man will say anything to save his neck. But Abram believed him and that was good enough for me. We cut him loose on the promise he'd hightail it back to his people at Warm Springs.

I fixed up a proper sign to let anyone who happened by know that these scoundrels was horse thieves and we left them there to be found by the Rangers or whatever posse might be trailing them.

A few days later Abram and I parted as friends and by God brothers. He was headed for Apache Pass where he hoped to trade tales with his ancestors and I had a date with a pretty lady and a gentleman named Holliday in the border town of Tombstone. It was a right proper name for that town but that's another story.

As I've told many a man, Abram Lincoln was one of the most honorable men, white, brown or red, I ever ran across in the Wild West. I owe him my life and I reckon he owes me his. For twelve or thirteen days on the trail in the old Southwest we was brothers. I'll stand by that till the day I day I die – which should be any day now.

BANDITO BROTHERS

My name is Chico Martinez. Over there by that mule is my brother Juan. He goes to the market to buy provisions. He does the walking and I do the talking.

This is our little farm. We grow beans and give them to the landowner who sells them to the market and gives us enough to fill our bellies and buy a bottle of tequila to kill the boredom that is our lives.

It was not always like this. Once we were notorious banditos! Very bad hombres and very good at it. I laugh! Most people around here do not believe me. But I tell you, senor, it is the truth. We ran horses from Chihuahua to Texas and New Mexico. We robbed travelers along the trail – mostly gamblers, Indians and stupid Mexicanos. We killed many men. Some for gold and horses, others because we did not like the way the looked at us. We were sensitive!

One time I captured an Apache scout. He was hiding in the Chiricahua Mountains. His people were all gone. They were herded onto a reservation like sheep. He was hungry and when he tried to steal some food from our camp I caught him red handed.

My people do not like the Apache. They are very good at lying and stealing and killing – almost as good as us. They killed my uncle and took his wife and daughter. I wanted to kill this man for my uncle but I got an idea.

These mountains have many trails and many places to hide from the law. The Apache knows them all. So I trained this man like a dog. We found someone who spoke his language and told him what we wanted him to do. When he did right we fed him. When he did wrong we beat him. Sometimes we just beat him. After a while he did right almost all the time. When we slept we tied him up like a pig and put a leash around his neck. After a while he did not try to get away.

Many times the Apache dog saved us from the law. We became very bold. We would steal horses with the Texas Rangers so close by they could reach out and touch us. We dared them to chase us into the mountains where we knew they could never find us. I hate the Rangers. I liked making fools of them.

But one time we were running horses up from Chihuahua when we came across a camp on the Pecos. There was no one by the fire. They hid when they heard us riding up. It was an ambush but we did not care. We were very drunk. I rode into their camp and yelled: Show yourselves, you stinking cowards!

They did. There were five of them. I killed two and my brother killed one but they had a gunfighter who killed two stupid Americanos and shot my brother in the arm. When my guns ran out of bullets we had to surrender. They tied us up and left us for the Rangers but we got loose.

I remember there was an Apache with a crippled leg who let the Apache dog go free. He was long gone by the time I could get my hands free to untie us. My brother lost a lot of blood. He was weak so I found our horses and we went back to Chihuahua. When my brother healed he did not want to be a bandito any more. He lost the taste for it. So we became the farmers we are today.

We were lucky that night on the Pecos. I still wonder why that gunfighter did not kill us. I would have. I could tell he wanted to kill us. It was in his eyes.

I think it was that Apache cripple. There was something about him – almost like a preacher. He was quiet and forgiving. It seemed he pitied us – especially his Apache brother.

Who knows? But I believe he saved our lives.

It is a funny world.

It doesn't matter. I still hate the Apache and the Apache still hate me. It does not change.

MISSOURI FARM BOYS

My brother Jacob and me, we was just farm boys from Missouri. Plain and simple folk. We grew up farming. Sharecropping. Then my daddy got the itch and we moved out Kansas way. We staked our own piece of land and commenced prairie farming. We did alright until the rain stopped, the wind kicked up and the land dried out to the point that it looked like the crust of mama's sweet potato pie.

By that time mama had a baby girl. Seems like the wind brought the sickness with it. The doc called it cholera. It took the baby first and took mama not long after.

There weren't much reason to stay on after that. Papa took to grieving and went half crazy. Looking back on it, I really believe he wanted to die but he was strong as a mule and twice as stubborn. There weren't no talking to him.

So finally me and Jacob hooked up with some wagons out of St. Louis and headed west. They was Mormons and we was not so after a spell we went our own way. We ended up in Denver, Colorado. It was a wild town and we was the sorriest looking cowboys that ever hit the trail, two grown men on one old mare, looking like we stepped off the farm – which of course we had.

I'm sure they seen us coming and had a good laugh about it 'cause they knew what we was up against. We picked up odd jobs and spent what little we made twice as fast as we could make it. Whoring, gambling, whiskey, what have you. For a while it seemed like we was having a good old time but our clothes was getting ragged and we was getting about as rank as a man can get. We hadn't had a bath, a decent meal or a roof over our heads in many a month. Got to the point even the whores looked the other way.

Long story short, we took to thieving. Seemed we finally found something we was halfway good at. We thieved anything that wasn't tied down and guarded through the night: guns, bullets, knives, tobacco, coffee, clothes, beaver pelts, buffalo hides. You name it, we thieved it. We found us a couple of boys who'd run our goods out of town, sell them somewheres else and come back with our shares. We had ourselves a business.

Miracle of miracles, we never did caught. The sheriff run us out of town on account of us being no good of mind or character. Lucky thing, too. We'd surely been hanged or shot or worse if we'd stayed. As it was, we were staked to a couple of horses, new duds, a couple of rifles and sharp shooting pistols.

That was the start of our lives as outlaws and it were beginning to look like our mama and papa was wrong: Thieving pays a lot better than farming. Course we knew it were wrong. We was raised to know the difference between right and wrong. But we was desperate men. Desperadoes. We did what we had to do.

We spent a good ten year hooking up with one gang or another, raiding horses, rustling cattle, holdups, stagecoach robberies. We was lucky. We felt like we couldn't lose. Oh, we was locked up a few times – getting drunk, shooting up a whorehouse, raising hell – but never for thieving. They'd just lock us up for the night and run us out of town the next day.

We kept moving south until we finally ended up in old Mexico where we signed on with the bandito brothers Juan and Chico Martinez. They was running horses up to Texas and New Mexico, holding up anyone they came across. They had themselves this Apache scout. Kept him drunk and tied up at night so he wouldn't take off. That Injun knew every trail and hideout in Apacheria and they used him to dodge the

Rangers or any posse that tried to track them. We'd just head for the mountains and that was that.

Well, that was how it went until we was trailing a string of horses up the Pecos. We come up on a camp late at night. There weren't much moonlight but the coals was still hot and glowing so we could see their horses tied up by the river. But there was no one in sight. It looked to me like an ambush so I suggested we hightail it out of there but those Mexicans was already off their horses. Chico was raising hell, daring them boys to come out and fight like men. We was drinking more than we should have and I believe that was our downfall.

All of sudden a shot rings out, Chico's sombrero goes flying and it sounds like we're surrounded by a whole tribe of Injuns. I dern near wet myself. Then someone yells out to drop our guns and I'm fixing to do just that when gunfire breaks out everywhere. When the smoke clears brother Jake is moaning like a stuck pig, gut shot, and the rest of us have our hands in the air, shaking like leaves in an autumn wind.

Turned out they was only two of them, a white gunfighter and an Injun with a crooked leg. They hogtied us, scattered our horses and threw our guns in the river. They left us there for the coyotes to feast on or the Rangers to find us. Luckily, Juan was a slippery weasel and he wriggled loose and untied us. Took half the day to hunt down our mounts and by then it was too late for Jacob. Seems our luck had run out.

Now brother Jake was a good old boy but he was never too bright. Why, he'd have followed me over the ledge of Grand Canyon if I told him we'd make it across. It was up to me to take care of him and I failed. I take responsibility and it weighs on me right heavy. I buried him down there by the Pecos and said a prayer that we might be forgiven.

Naturally the Apache got away. Me and the Mexicans split up. We was nothing but bad luck together. I considered myself lucky they didn't shoot me for the clothes I was wearing. Turns out there is honor among thieves.

JACK RANDOM

I went back to Kansas to seek a quiet kind of life. By a miracle of the most unlikely chance, turns out my papa was still alive. The rains came back and we made a go of the old family farm. That was the end of my desperado days. It was good for a spell but in the end it cost me my brother. That ain't a fair deal in any man's life.

WARM SPRINGS MEDICINE MAN

I am Mimbres Apache and a man who listens to the spirit world. My hands hold the knowledge of healing, my heart contains the ways of the ancestors, and my eyes carry the history of my people.

My knowledge was given to me by my father who was also a man of the spirit world. In the summer of the white eyes year eighteen hundred and ninety, the year when the Ghost Dance spread across the plains, my father was an old man as I am today, living on the Warm Springs Reservation in New Mexico. The people were poor. There was not enough food, not enough blankets, no medicine and not enough hope to feed the soul.

In that summer of sorrow my father told me about a man who came from Indian Territory, a Kiowa Apache pilgrim who was on his way to visit Wavoka, the founder of the Ghost Dance. I was a young man who knew nothing. I did not see this man or if I did I did not care. Like most of my people, I saw only a man with a crooked leg and avoided him. My father recognized him as a man of the spirit world, a messenger from the ancestors and the Great Spirit itself.

He offered a message of hope but we could not hear his words. We were broken spirits, half of what we were and no longer true Apaches.

The Apache are a superstitious people. At that time we believed a deformity was the mark of an evil spirit. Often those born with deformities were allowed to die. Sometimes death was given to them. We believed they would be made whole in the next world.

So my people saw this man's clubfoot and we were afraid. We did not look in his eyes. We feared he brought disease and sickness. We believed his blessing was a curse and his message was death.

My father listened to his words and spoke to him. We had heard of the Ghost Dance but we had never spoken to a man who danced and chanted the sacred words.

My father saw that his spirit was good. He looked into his eyes and felt good will and wisdom, the hope and seed of sacred power. He gave him a medicine bundle to give him strength and protect him from harm on his journey. He asked that he give it to Wavoka as a sacred offering.

In this way the people of the Mimbres Apache Warm Springs Reservation joined in the Ghost Dance though few of us would ever know.

Now, every year I go to Wounded Knee and I remember my father and the pilgrim with a clubfoot and I believe in the Ghost Dance. It is not what the white man feared. It is not a dance of war and death. It is a call to the people to remember the old ways, to hold on to our culture and spiritual beliefs, to remain who we have always been, separate and apart from the white society. We were meant to walk the red road with pride and dignity.

I saw him once at Wounded Knee. He was an old man, very wise, and held the knowledge of the old ways in his heart. He possessed the gift of healing. He did not remember me but I told him my father's words and asked him to forgive my people for how they treated him.

He said he understood the people of Warm Springs. It was a time of great suffering. He was pleased I had recovered my spirit and he gave me his blessing. We sweated together and smoked the sacred pipe. He was too old to dance but he taught me the steps and many songs of the Ghost Dance.

He taught us that there are good people among the white eyes – just as there are many among the red skinned people who would betray us. He taught that we are all one before the mother, the father and the Great Spirit.

His name was Black Crow. His medicine was strong. He is a great man who will always live in the heart of the Apache people.

BRUSH IN THE WIND

I didn't start out to be a saloon gal, a woman serving the base needs of men, a common main street whore. There are occasions when a lady has no more control over her destiny than sagebrush in the wind.

If I had it all to do again I never would have fallen for a slick, smooth talking gambling man with an eye for pretty ladies and the spirit of adventure. His name was Jimmy Cole. He was a right handsome man dressed all in black with a white lace shirt and his Bat Masterson hat.

I met him at a social in Chicago and fell to his charms like a dozen girls before me. I felt like the belle of the ball when he asked for my hand. He introduced me to the nightlife, the saloons and the gambling houses that never closed.

The year was 1875. I was young and pretty and we were as happy as children in a field of wildflowers on a warm sunny day. He never tired of telling me how much he loved me, how I was his lucky charm. I swore I'd follow him anywhere. Two years later anywhere turned out to be Denver, Colorado. He'd read about the grand saloons and gambling houses of the west – especially Denver and San Francisco. So we sold our belongings and boarded a train out west. We planned a week or two in Denver before we would move on to San Francisco. After that we'd decide where we wanted to live.

Plans have an awkward way of going awry.

Denver was an exciting town with a spirit all its own. It was unlike anything we'd ever experienced. Things went well at first. We got a room at the finest hotel. It was a bit rustic but not at all as bad as we'd been told.

I stayed out of the gambling halls until Jimmy had a run of bad luck and asked me to go along with him for luck. He was sure I could help him turn it around and I was flattered that he thought so.

One look around and I knew he was overmatched but how do you tell the man you love he doesn't measure up? You do not.

His luck only got worse. I finally took a job in the saloon to pay the hotel bill and Jimmy continued to lose. He was on one of his famous losing streaks and a real bastard to be around. To say that he abused me would hardly be an adequate description. But I loved that man and I stood by him. I suppose I considered it a test of my devotion. Honestly, the alternatives were not very appealing.

One morning I woke up and Jimmy was gone. He sold most of my jewelry and boarded the train for San Francisco. He didn't even bother to leave a note. I imagine he blamed me for his turn of luck. In truth I was not entirely sorry to see him go. But I was sorry he sold my jewelry.

I had just enough left that I might have taken a train home to Chicago or on to San Francisco. I did not wish to arrive in San Francisco penniless but neither did I wish to return home a disgrace and a failure. I loathed the thought of having to hear the muffled "I told you so" or "poor girl" or expressions of false sympathy. I preferred to remain in Denver though I soon realized that the wages of a saloon girl were hardly sufficient to keep me in fashion. As a woman of culture, I was accustomed to attending theater, musical entertainments and art galleries. These were the things that gave my life meaning – a rich and full experience.

I had but two alternatives that would allow the standard of living I desired: I could find a gentleman of means to support me or I could indulge a number of gentlemen for a fee. At the time and under the circumstances, the latter appeared to me more palatable.

We are not always blessed with the foresight to see the consequences of our decisions until it is too late to alter them. Some decisions are irreversible and nothing we can do or say will turn the clock back to former, more innocent times.

I made mistakes. I have regrets.

Looking back from the distant place I find myself today, I realize all might have been well had I not taken the advice of a gentleman with a fine reputation for business. I invested much of my savings in a herd of Texas Longhorns. I was assured of a healthy profit but the winter was fierce and the cattle died. In an instant all those years of indulging men's fancy went for nothing. I was once again penniless and the beauty of my youth had withered on the vine.

I lost my position at the saloon to a younger, prettier girl. I moved from the hotel to a brothel that catered to workingmen. As the years rolled by I began to serve the clients the younger girls would not take: the vilest of men and those of darker skin tones. I preferred the latter.

There are things I did during those desperate years I would not tell anyone. It ended when finally I swallowed my pride and wrote my sister in Chicago. She sent me enough for a ticket home. Out of pity or perhaps genuine kindness my family provided for my needs.

The only price I would be compelled to pay were the prying eyes and invasive questions I cheerfully entertained at family gatherings. The children were excused from the room and I told them the story of my years in Denver.

The only consolation was the knowledge that I could endure absolutely anything. I thank God my mother was no longer alive.

FIRE AT THE HJ CORRAL

I. Crow Man.

I was among the first of the Crow tribe to embrace the Ghost Dance. I journeyed to the Paiute camp, spoke with the prophet Wavoka, and promised to spread his word to the northern tribes – the Lakota, Arapaho, Blackfoot, Cheyenne and Comanche. It was a promise I kept for seven seasons of the sun.

In the summer of the white man's year 1890, when the Ghost Dance was in practice everywhere and yet nearing its final days, I heard a different calling.

As more and more Indians took the train on pilgrimage to the prophet's cam on the eastern side of the Nevada's, more and more left their horses in cities such as Denver, Cheyenne and Salt Lake to be cared for until they returned from their journey on the Iron Horse. When they returned, however, many found their horses gone – sold or traded by the stable owners who had no honor.

I went to Denver to see what could be done. The law was of no help. "One or two horses," the sheriff said, "an innocent mistake."

I learned that the lawmen received money from the horse traders. Their method was simple. They did not steal every horse – only the finest and those that were not branded or the brands were easily altered. At night they would run the horses out of town where traders waited to buy them at a low price. They would take them far away to be sold again at a profit. When the Indian returned for his horse he was offered a broken down nag. When the Indian protested the stable owner would wave his arms and call for the law. The lawmen would always say the same thing: An innocent mistake. He should take the horse he is offered.

I decided what could be done. Not all the stables in Denver were crooked. I warned the Indians not to take their horses to the crooked ones. Of course, I could not be in many places at one time so I gathered a small group of Indians from different tribes to help. Some would work or hunt to provide for our needs while others stood watch over the stables. We set up camp outside of town.

McPherson's Corral and Stables was the worst of them. McPherson hated Indians and many lost their horses to his treachery. He would smile and promise to take special care and the Indian would believe him.

I directed many pilgrims to the stables of a man named Henry Johnson. He was an honest man, a black man and a man of honor. He charged a fair price and he always kept his word.

For a time things went well. I warned many pilgrims and Mr. Johnson gained many customers. McPherson heard what was happening and he grew very angry. He threatened me many times. When he called the law my friends would warn me and I would slip away. Finally he took matters into his own hands.

Late at night his men released Johnson's horses and set fire to his stables. The fire spread to his blacksmith shop and living quarters. Mr. Johnson managed to save himself and some of his belongings but his business, along with everything he had built and worked for, was gone.

We rounded up some of the horses that were trusted to his care but most had vanished into the night. Everyone knew McPherson had done this thing but there was little we could do. Should we have burned his stables? Should we have stolen his horses?

APACHE JACK

Denver was the kind of town that would kill ten Indians for the act of one. They hated us and blamed us for every theft and murder. They blamed us for everything wrong with their city and their lives. We did not wish to see many die so there was nothing we could do.

I apologized to Mr. Johnson as he prepared to leave for Oregon country. He would not hear of it. He thanked me for what I had done and wished me good fortune.

"You are not to blame for what the white man does."

I returned to my people on the reservation and swore I would never go among the white people again. It is a promise I have kept.

II. Jeffrey McPherson.

We McPherson's are a hard working, hard driving, hard drinking and hard living lot. I was born to the pioneer spirit. When the great iron lady in New York harbor cried out from across the sea, "Give me your tired, poor and adventurous spirits," we McPherson's answered the call. When old Horace Greeley ushered forth the call, "Go west, young man!" we answered once again.

History will show that this wondrous continent of North America was destined to become the last great bastion of freedom in all this world and the only thing that stood in our way was the lowest breed of human savages known to mankind. Those who wax poetic about the "noble savage" have never seen what I've seen: the bodies of soldiers and dead settlers, their scalps removed, heads severed and private parts removed for war trophies.

I agree with the honorable Colonel John Chivington that the only good Indian is a dead Indian. So I was there when we shot the last buffalo and sent the savages to confinement on reservations. I was there when we drove the last spike in the coffin of the so-called Native American at Promontory Point. I was there when we pushed through the Dawes Act, opening Indian lands to white settlers. And I was there when we killed Sitting Bull and Crazy Horse and drove the Sioux from their precious Black Hills.

"Manifest destiny!" That's the cry of all right thinking and God fearing people. One country from the Atlantic to the Pacific led by the most enlightened folks on the face of this earth! A nation of Christ! The removal of the Indian was preordained. It is the work of a wise if sometimes harsh God – no more, no less.

Now when you ask me about the summer of 1890 I cringe to think what the lily white naysayers who never did an honest day's labor might have told you: that I, Jeffrey McPherson, would stoop so low as to thieving horses from Indians! That by God is the fox blaming the lamb for raiding the chicken coop! As for burning another man's place of business, I swear upon my mother's grave I never done and never would do such a thing.

The truth is I was minding my own business, tending to my own stables. My customers came in all sizes and colors and I treated them right as rain. But a rumor went about that I was cheating them redskins, trading their good horses for old nags. If that were true I would have been thrown in jail or run out of town. The fact is I was never charged with any crime but the rumor persisted and I lost a lot of customers to a man of color by the name of Henry Johnson.

That particular summer there was a tremendous rush of Indians taking the train from Denver to Paiute country out west. Said they were pilgrims and their newfound religion was something called the Ghost Dance. They were trying to raise the dead. The point is I had a good number of Indian customers before the rumor and after I had none. Business suffered. My family suffered.

Mr. Johnson prospered from my misfortune. Now I can't say for sure who started the rumor but the scriptures say: Look to he who profits from sin.

Naturally when his stables burned down the suspicion fell

on me. I was questioned and cleared by the law. I tell you like I told them: All I did, as I had every right to do, was tell a few of my friends about my situation. Now if someone took it in his mind to take some action of his own accord, that's between him and his God. I told the truth and that's the end of it.

I will say this: When Mr. Johnson left Denver was better off for it. It's no secret that I am not a friend of the dark skinned races. History will show that the worst mistake America ever made was the importation of African slaves. Mr. Johnson took honest work from hard working white folk and he paid the price.

Of course things did not work out so well for me in the end. I had a string of bad luck. Maybe that Injun Joe, an evil Crow medicine man, put a hex on me and mine. Who can tell? We ought to have put a rope to his neck but, being law-abiding men, we let him go his way just like any other man in the city. If anything, we were far too lenient.

All's I know is: I lost pretty much everything and took to the bottle just like so many lost souls before me. So now I tend bar at a rundown saloon. That's life and so be it. You won't hear Jeffrey McPherson bellyaching about it. Not like some men I know.

III. Henry Johnson.

I am a free Negro. I was freed by the Emancipation Proclamation in the war between the north and the south. I fought for the Union Army in the all-Negro regiment. I paid the price for my freedom.

When the war ended, like hundreds and thousands of other Negroes, I went west where it was said a man could work hard, live free and make a decent living. I mined gold in California, scouted for wagon trains on the Oregon Trail, hunted buffalo on the great plains, herded Longhorns from the Rio Grande to Big Sky Country and laid tracks for the

Northern Pacific Railroad.

I taught myself to read and write. I never drank, never whored and never gambled so I was able to save a little here and there until I had enough money to start my own stables and blacksmith shop in Denver, Colorado.

I chose Denver for two reasons: First, in all my travels I never saw a more majestic sight than the Great Rocky Mountains. Second, it had a need. They had their share of stables and blacksmiths but none of them served anyone but white folks. Denver was a major thoroughfare and there were many free Negroes, Mexicans and Indians coming through that could use my services. So I got a silent partner, a white man who signed the papers, and bought a parcel of land on the outskirts of town. I built my home, my shop, my corral and stables with my own two hands. I didn't ask for help and none was offered. After a time, word got around and I built up a clientele.

After the railroads were established and the Ghost Dance worked its way across the plains, more and more Indians of all tribes came from the south and west to Denver. They'd leave their horses here and take the train to the Paiute camp where the Ghost Dance founder lived. They were pilgrims. That's what they called themselves and who am I to argue?

By that time some of the other stables opened to non-whites. They saw there was money in it. Unfortunately, some of them were crooked. They would take the Indian's horse, run it out of town and sell it or trade it for goods. The law was in on it so there wasn't much they could do.

In the summer of 1890 a man known to us as Injun Joe took it upon himself to warn the pilgrims about the crooked stables. He sent many of them my way. Looking back, I wish he had sent them to one of the honest stables run by a white man. It would have been better for everyone involved.

There was a man named McPherson. He was the worst of the crooked lot. I was told and I believe it that he was a member of a secret society of the Ku Klux Klan. I know for a fact he hated Negroes and he hated Indians almost as much. I have no doubt he was a horse thief.

When my place went up in flames everyone knew who did it but I only had two choices: Kill him and hang for it or leave town and start a new life. I came as close to being hanged as any man can but I chose to live.

I remember what my mama told me on the day I headed west: "They can take your money and they can take your home but as long as you've got your freedom, they can't take your pride."

I headed for Oregon territory and I did well. I married a good strong woman from the Yakima tribe. She was a Ghost Dancer. We would have three children whose skin is the finest shade of dark tan you'd ever want to see.

Our children take care of us now. Of course, we have our share of problems but I've learned that most folks are good people once they get past the surface of things. We live a good life. I wouldn't trade it for all the gold in Denver.

ARAPAHO SPIRIT GUIDE

I am White Wolf of the Arapaho. My people once camped far to the north where the white wolf lived. The wolf is wise and clever. The name was a great honor handed down to me by my fathers and grandfathers.

The land on which Laramie, Cheyenne, Denver and North Platte now sit was once Arapaho land. With our brothers and sisters of the Cheyenne tribe we roamed freely what is now Colorado, Wyoming, Nebraska and Kansas. We were here long before the white man ever dream of this land.

We hunted buffalo with reverence and care. We never wished to kill all the buffalo like the white man did. We depended on the buffalo for food, shelter and clothing. When we killed the buffalo we gave thanks and paid tribute that the buffalo would return to us.

We warred with our enemies, the Shoshone and Crow, but we fought with honor. We never wished to kill all our enemies for we depended on them for honor and manhood. When we killed our enemies we paid tribute to their courage and honor as warriors.

But the white man came and killed for sport and game. The time came when there were no more buffalo. They declared war on all native tribes and soon, I fear, there will be no more native people. We treat the land as sacred. The white treats it as property. He lays waste to the land, digging and scratching for his precious metals. He pumps poison into the air and water. Pretty soon I fear there will be no more trees and plants and living beings who depend on the land will die.

APACHE JACK

This is why my people embraced the Ghost Dance and the vision of its founder, the prophet Wavoka. He promised an end to the white man's rule, the return of the buffalo and the rebirth of the ancestors on earth.

I was not the first of my tribe to do pilgrimage. At first I was reserved in judgment. I did not believe yet I did not disbelieve. I waited until I saw the hope it gave my people and then I became a Ghost Dancer.

The elders chose me for pilgrimage. I decided to walk from the Wind River Reservation in central Wyoming to Cheyenne on the southern Wyoming border. There I would board the train to the Paiute camp in eastern Nevada.

On the long walk I stayed far away from the white man's path and each night I chanted and prayed for a vision. On the fourth night I made camp on sacred ground. It was open land but there was an outcrop of stone, like a small mountain, with a flat round surface on top. I knew there had been a great battle here and I could feel the presence of the many warriors who died.

I filled my hands with soil and climbed to the top. I drew a circle and gave my offering to the four directions. I placed my medicine bundle in the center of the circle and cleansed my spirit with sage. I smoked from the sacred pipe and began to chant. Soon I found myself at a distant place where the ground was made of cloud and there was no earth. I saw many of my people, some familiar, some dead. I asked where I could find Wavoka and the people pointed the way.

I came to a man with sadness in his eyes who said: I am Wavoka. We sat and smoked from his pipe. I asked if he was a spirit being.

"I am a man like you," he said.

I asked about the Ghost Dance and the prophecies he had promised the people of many tribes.

"I tell them what they want to hear. I give them what they need to survive. Is it wrong to do so? The people chant and dance. Their spirits soar! Hope lives in their hearts.

Where there were a hundred tribes divided, now there is one tribe, one people united."

He drew from his pipe and watched the smoke rise before he spoke. I looked around and saw the spirits of the buffalo, the elk, the wolf and the deer. I saw the eagle and hawk soar in great sweeping circles. I saw a river as clear and pure as it must have been before the two legs walked the earth. It was a vision of beauty, peace and harmony. It brought tears of sacred joy to my eyes.

"The ancestors will not return," he said, "except in our hearts and in our memories. The white man will not go but we may yet survive as a people."

The vision faded and I was back on the mountaintop staring at a sky of many stars. I was pleased to be back on the earth but my heart was heavy with the knowledge that Wavoka had given me. When I boarded the train in Cheyenne I did not intend to share my vision. Wavoka had many detractors and I did not wish to be identified with these men. It was sacred knowledge and needed to be regarded with great care.

But I found myself seated next to a young man of the Kiowa Apache who had special powers, his own sacred knowledge and a hunger for the truth. His mind was not yet clouded with the thoughts of his elders. I sensed that he too held a secret vision. So I spoke to this man whose name was Black Crow. I spoke as an old man speaks to a child with special gifts. I spoke of my vision and the words Wavoka had spoken. He asked why I still made pilgrimage. I said that I needed to look into Wavoka's eyes and see for myself. Then I would be sure. I told him I still believed the Ghost Dance was good for the native peoples.

Then he told me his vision. He described a place of desolation where the white man's smoke blocked the sun. I told him I had seen such a place. It was called Butte, Montana, where the white man mined and worked metals with great fires that always burned.

APACHE JACK

He spoke of many soldiers with cannons and guns surrounding a Ghost Dance and killing all: men, women and children. He spoke of the ancestors on a path to the Overworld, a path that vanished when he tried to follow.

I knew he had seen the truth.

We traveled together to Wavoka's camp and together we looked into the prophet's eyes. We saw the truth and we knew that Wavoka knew what we had seen. He was a man, just a man trapped by his own words and his own creation. The Ghost Dance became bigger than the dreamer who created it and he could not turn back.

I returned to my people and shared with them the knowledge I was given. Some believed me. Others did not. But when news of Wounded Knee came to Wind River, they knew the truth of my vision. I thought of the young Kiowa Apache pilgrim who foresaw the massacre and wondered what became of him.

I asked the Great Spirit to protect him and guide him on his journey. I prayed that he survived to become a spirit guide to his people. He had the healing power.

As for me, I devoted myself to keeping the old ways alive – the healing ways, the sacred rites, the ancient beliefs. I have lived long enough to see the fruits of my efforts and those of others who joined in this cause. It is a good life when there is hope. When there is no hope, there is no life at all.

THE GATHERING

The gathering at Wavoka's camp in the summer of 1890 was the greatest event of my life. Never have I seen so many tribes come together as one people, in peace and harmony, united by their belief in one man and his vision: the vision that became known as the Ghost Dance.

Old enemies sat down together and smoked the sacred pipe. The Cheyenne and Shoshone, Arapaho and Lakota, Blackfoot and Comanche, Kiowa and Crow all came together as one tribe, sharing songs and stories, chanting and singing and dancing in the sacred circle.

I was honored to hear Wavoka speak. His words were powerful. The white man says he preached destruction and death but it is not Wavoka but the white man who practiced these things. When a man is evil he sees evil in others.

Wavoka spoke of peace and honor. He spoke of keeping the old ways alive within us. He spoke of being one with mother earth and father sky and all the creatures that inhabit the land, the air and water. He spoke of white people who were not like the soldiers and agents who lied and cheated us. He asked us to reach out to these white people for they also were our brothers and sisters.

"Only in unity can we be strong. Only as one people can we survive."

I met many people of many tribes at the gathering and many became friends. But one man stands out in the memories of my heart. His name was Black Crow but many knew him as Crooked Leg for he was born with one leg that pointed inward. He was Kiowa Apache and came from

Indian Territory.

In other camps the people would have avoided Black Crow, seeing only his crooked leg and not his true spirit, but in Wavoka's camp he was welcome. We shared many stories, talked of many things and became close friends. I still remember the words to his song when we danced the Ghost Dance:

Oh Great Spirit, hear my prayer
I listen to the wind
I look for signs in all things
I bow my head to Mother Earth
Oh Great Spirit, let me be wise!

He was already wise for such a young man. He told me about the Oklahoma Land Rush. He said the white man would take more and more land from all native peoples and he was right. He said they would take the best hunting ground and he was right. He said we would be forced to live by the white man's charity and we would lose our pride and he was right.

In my heart I knew the truth of his words but I did not want to believe. I told him Wavoka's prophecy would come to pass: The Great Spirit would rise to the red man's cause. Father Sky would open with the crack of thunder and wash the soldiers away. Mother Earth would rumble, shake and swallow them whole. Then, when the earth was cleansed and the soldiers were dead, the world would be born again. The buffalo would return. The four legs and the winged brothers and sisters would return and the land would heal from the white man's wounds.

He told me he liked my words and he would pray for the truth of them but I knew he did not believe. Finally, he told me of his friend who had seen Wavoka in a vision. He said Wavoka was not a spirit being but only a man. He was a good man who wanted to give the people hope and strength but his prophecies would not come to pass.

He then spoke of his own vision, a vision he did not understand until he spoke to the spirit guide he had met on the train. It revealed to him the white man's destruction of the earth, the last days of the Ghost dance in a bloody massacre and the path to the Overworld.

"It is a place of greater beauty than any man can imagine. It is a place where Wavoka's prophecies have already come to be. It is a place the ancestors will not leave. Why should they? They have already lived their lives on this earth."

Again, I knew the truth of his words but I did not want to believe them.

When Black Crow returned to his people before the first snow I went with him to Denver. That is where we left our horses when we took the train to Wavoka's camp. But when we reached Denver our horses were gone – stolen by the white men we paid good money to care for them. They offered me an old hag that was sick and dying and I refused. It would not have survived the journey. They offered my friend nothing – not even an apology. They said there was a fire. It was an act of God. Nothing they could do.

We have come to know the white man's God: He does not like Indians.

Soon the first snow would fall from the sky. Already there was a chill in the air. My friend lived far to the south. With his leg he was slow on foot. He would not survive so I asked him to stay with my people for the winter and he accepted.

We made it to the Cheyenne camp before the first snow. At first my people did not wish to welcome him but they saw how I felt and soon they respected him as I did.

It was a long hard winter. The winds swept across the land, howling like ancient wolves and the cold settled in our bones like the icy stare of soldiers. Black Crow spent many hours alone in silence. Many times he fasted and cried for wisdom and guidance in the cold, lonely night.

I told my people of his vision and we feared.

When a Lakota rider came from the north we took him in, gave him food and comfort. With eyes of deep sorrow, he told us what happened at Wounded Knee. Hundreds of Ghost Dancers – men, women and children – lay dead on the frozen ground. The blue coats fired their guns with many bullets that did not need reloading. The people ran but the creek and the hills blocked the way. The soldiers tracked them down and killed everyone they could find.

I felt numb. It was not Wavoka who had seen the future; it was my friend Black Crow. It was exactly as his vision foretold.

When the long winter finally gave way, we held a ceremony for the Ghost Dancers of Wounded Knee and honored Black Crow for his vision of truth. We asked his blessing and gave him a good horse for his journey home.

Many years later, on pilgrimage to Wounded Knee, I saw Black Crow again. His eyes shined with new hope for the future and the young people who would guide the way.

"The Ghost Dance is still alive," he said with a wink and a broad smile.

The young people with him respected their elders and asked many questions. It has not always been so. Their visit was a precious gift for there is nothing that so warms a heart like hope born anew.

We talked through the night and parted knowing we would not see each other again on this good earth.

The Prophet Wavoka circa 1892
Probable Photographer James Mooney

WAVOKA OF THE PAIUTE

I am Wavoka of the Paiute.

I was once a spokesman for all native peoples. My words soared as the eagle. The prayers and the dance I taught the people spread across the land. Pilgrims from all tribes came to me wanting to know more of my vision, thirsting for my words, pleading for knowledge of their ancestors, asking my blessings and receiving what wisdom I could offer. I told them what I had seen in a visit to the Overworld, the world of the ancestors and the Great Spirit, but they always wanted more.

Everything changed when the soldiers killed Sitting Bull and hundreds of the Oglala, Hunkpapa and Minneconjou Sioux as they danced the sacred dance and chanted the sacred songs of the Ghost Dance at Wounded Knee.

Was I responsible?

Many blame me for what the soldiers did. But it was not I who fired the Hotchkiss guns. It was not the Ghost Dance that put murder in the hearts of the white man. It was there long before Wavoka walked the earth.

But I mourn for my people.

Now I am all but forgotten and the Ghost Dance is swept away like dust on the open prairie.

As I look back I wonder what I could have done. I should have trained my messengers more carefully. I should have spoken more clearly. Many things were said that were not true. Words were put into my mouth by well meaning followers who may have wanted to please their own tribes.

I did not give the sacred shirts to the Sioux. I never said

the Ghost Dancers were immune to the white man's bullets. I never said nor did I desire that all white men should die. I never said that our ancestors would return to this world in the flesh. I never said I was a spirit being, the messiah or the Son of God.

But my words were translated to a hundred different tribes with a hundred different tongues and each heard what they wanted to hear.

I still believe my vision was sacred and true. The buffalo will return and multiply. The white man and his great society will be ravaged by the shaking earth, fire and wind. Floods will cover the land and the white man's machines will fail and rust.

Those among us who still believe and who remember the old ways will survive the mass destruction. People of all races will come to us for shelter and the sacred knowledge of survival. We will answer in wisdom and in kindness. We will welcome them and form a new society where all our people can live in harmony, where the elders and the earth mother are respected and cared for as a way of life, where all are free to live and worship in their own way.

But the people have no patience. They want the new world now – in our lifetime. They do not understand that in the eyes of the Great Spirit we are as leaves on a fast moving stream. We pass in the blink of an eye. But that which we hold in our hearts and hand to our children lives forever. Our spirits survive. Always.

These things I have prophesied will come to pass though Wavoka will not be among the living to see them. The people must prepare. For I have spoken truly the vision that was given me by the Great Spirit. That is all I can tell you.

Go now and leave an old man to die in peace.

LAKOTA RIDER

To the young people of the Lakota nation everything begins with Wounded Knee. But I remember a time when everything we lived for and held in our hearts ended at Wounded Knee.

I remember when Sitting Bull still walked the earth with pride and courage. I remember when the last herd of buffalo walked over the mountain at Bear Butte. I remember when the Iron Horse and the spotted cow came to this land. I remember General Custer at the Greasy Grass. I remember when the sacred Black Hills belonged to the people.

But when I dream the dream of darkness it is always Wounded Knee. When I sweat in the sacred sweat lodge I remember Wounded Knee. And when the young gather around my fire, they always say: Speak to us of Wounded Knee.

And so I tell them what I saw with my own eyes. I tell them as I told the people of many tribes in the winter of the white man's year eighteen hundred and ninety one. I tell them as I tell you now.

In the fall of the white man's year eighteen hundred and ninety the people of Pine Ridge and Rosebud reservations were divided. Many were afraid. They wanted peace at any cost. They lived close to the Agency where they received rations of food, blankets, coffee and favors the others did not receive. I was among the others who lived far from the Agency and the soldiers who guarded it so that we could live as we pleased and dance the forbidden dance.

We were Ghost Dancers and we were proud. We threw

away the white man's clothing and dressed in the old way. Our women sewed and painted the special shirts that the elders blessed with powerful medicine. We believed they would protect us from the white man's bullets. We wore the sacred shirts whenever we danced for we knew that the soldiers would come and we knew what they would do.

The agents told the great white fathers in Washington that the Indians were on the warpath and that the Ghost Dance was a war dance. Reporters came and wrote stories that the Indians were preparing for the final confrontation and that we would fight until the last warrior fell.

Many soldiers came with loaded guns and nervous trigger fingers but they found no war parties so they waited. More soldiers came with more guns and cannons to crush the great uprising. They looked at us with death in their eyes but we caused no trouble so still they waited.

We moved far from their camp, far from their view, far from their reporters and far from their soldiers of death, and we danced. We did not know that there were traitors among us who told the soldiers where we gathered to dance.

Winter had come to the Dakotas and General Miles was restless so they sent Lakota police, traitors to their own people, to arrest Sitting Bull at Standing Rock. They sent forty-three warriors to arrest one old man. They knew there would be trouble.

They rode into camp and announced their intentions. They wanted us to cry out in protest and we did not disappoint them. They did what they came to do. They shot an old man until the spirit left his body. Then they returned to their masters and told them the uprising had begun.

We were angry but we did not want war. We fled to Big Foot's camp in the north. The whites knew Big Foot as one who wanted peace. He took us in knowing there would be trouble. He knew we were not on the war path. Our crime was believing in the Ghost Dance.

When the soldiers came we told them we did not wish to

fight so they waited. They ordered us to camp in an open space with a creek and hills to our back. They promised they would not open fire.

Many of us were warriors. I ask: Would we have agreed to this if we wanted war? There was much heated talk but Big Foot said the soldiers would not open fire on a peaceful camp. So we agreed. We watched as the soldiers surrounded us and set up their cannons that fired many bullets and we were afraid. They ordered us to give up our weapons. We knew then we had made a grave error. Without our weapons we could not protect our women and children. But with their guns pointed at us and the creek and the hills blocking our escape, what choice did we have?

There was some commotion, loud arguments and shoving as they gathered our guns. Then, when all the guns had been taken, they opened fire and they kept firing until no man, woman or child was standing. Those who ran were tracked and killed. I saw an old woman with a child throw open her robe to show her sex and they killed them both like dogs and went on with their killing. Still, some escaped. I escaped. I lay still under several bodies by the creek side, covered in blood, and they passed me by.

I have read many of the white man's accounts of what happened at Wounded Knee. Some say a shot was fired. This is not true. The first and the first hundred shots fired came from the soldiers' Hotchkiss guns. Some say an old man threw dust in the air. Yes, this happened. But it happened long before the firing began. Why did the soldiers wait until we were disarmed?

For many years the white man speaks of honor at The Battle of Wounded Knee. There was no battle and there is no honor. There is only shame and sorrow.

Now there is talk of reparations. They offer gambling. I ask: What is the price of so many dead? We lost the best of our people. You offer gambling? Give us the Black Hills, and then we'll talk.

In the winter of the massacre at Wounded Knee, with the earth frozen and covered with snow, with the dead still lying on the open ground, I began the journey that would consume the rest of my life. What remained of my family said: Do not go. The soldiers will hunt you down and kill you! I said: The pain and the sorrow of Wounded Knee is great to hold in the hearts of so few. We must share it with all the native peoples so that the sorrow can be felt by all and remembered for all time.

So I rode to the Cheyenne camp, then the Shoshone and Comanche, and I kept riding until I came to Indian Territory. Everywhere I told what had happened and everywhere the people cried and mourned and honored the dead. They gave their promise never to forget. They promised to keep the old ways alive in their hearts where the white man's bullets cannot reach.

Today, as I near the end of my journey, I still tell the story. Always, when my telling is ended, I say: Do not forget those who died at Wounded Knee. They died for you. They died so that you will remember who you are as a people. They died so you will keep the old ways alive.

Do not forget.

WHITE MAN AT WOUNDED KNEE

"Hey white boy!"

I braced myself. The voice seemed familiar yet not familiar. All day long I'd been asking myself: What am I doing here? Some of the Indians were asking the same thing. I was beginning to feel like the only boy in a school for girls. So I would not be surprised if the hand I now felt on my shoulder intended no good.

"Two Feathers!"

He was a friend from back home in Nashville. Well, at least I called him a friend. I don't really know how he referred to me. I met him at a pow wow. I had been to his sweat lodge and we had exchanged thoughts at several gatherings. He was the spiritual leader of a circle of Cherokee and Choctaw who welcomed whites to their ceremonies. It was different here at Wounded Knee and Two Feathers was aware of my discomfort.

"Someone give you a hard time?"

"You could say that."

The fact is I had been asked to leave. The Lakota who did the asking told me the Ghost Dance was forbidden to whites. He said I would not be allowed to participate or witness. He said my presence offended the ancestors.

Two Feathers said: Wounded Knee has more meaning to the Lakota than to others. It was their people who died here.

"And my people who killed them."

It was his way not to answer the obvious. He let it pass like a soft breeze.

"This is sacred ground," he said, his eyes sweeping the

sky as if searching for a sign. "Some say only the full-blood Lakota should be allowed to walk it."

"They want you to leave too?"

He smiled. "If they did, I would not go. I know why I am here. I believe in connecting to the past. I believe that all native peoples should be as one. That was Wavoka's vision and it is mine as well."

"I share those beliefs – even if I am a white man."

"As I have said, not all whites are the same. We all understand that. We all want the same thing: To preserve our heritage, to keep the old ways alive, to be one with the ancestors and the Great Spirit. I say: an Indian is in the heart and mind."

"Some say it is in the blood."

He nodded and pointed to a small dot in the western sky. It was a hawk though I would not recognize it for some time.

"Brother Hawk brings a message."

He placed his hand on my shoulder and guided me down an embankment to where the people gathered around a fire to hear an old man speak. His name was Black Crow and he was known to all in the gathering as a Kiowa Apache spirit guide. He was a healer who had gone on pilgrimage to Wavoka's camp as a young man. He had smoked the sacred pipe with the founder of the Ghost Dance.

I noticed his clubfoot. It somehow seemed out of place. His eyes were deep and wise. I wanted nothing more than to hear this man speak but I was afraid his words were off limit to whites so I held back and wandered off. But Two Feathers gave me the courage to return and take my place in the circle surrounding Black Crow.

In the corner of my view I could see the Lakota man who asked me to leave glaring. I chose not to look back. It was early in a week of planned activities that would culminate with four days of the Ghost Dance. Only a year removed from the siege and showdown with the government that led to two Indian deaths and over forty arrests, the gathering would become political. But for now it was spiritual.

There were about three dozen of us in the circle. One third appeared to be full bloods, another third mixed bloods and remaining third were whites, Asians, African Americans and Hispanics. The old man looked at us as if we were a nation, representing all earth's children, his eyes glowing with pride as he rose.

"I have lived many cycles of the sun." His voice was deep and powerful, resonating in the nearby hills.

"These eyes have lived to see the return of the buffalo. They have witnessed the power of the earth mother to heal, to cleanse the air, water and land, so that the grass and trees may grow again, so that all creatures may live and thrive.

"But always I have longed to see the gathering that sits before me now for it is the seed of a new age. You, my friends, are the great hope of the future. This is what Wavoka saw in his vision. He welcomed all tribes, all colors, all races, united by their belief in the brotherhood of all beings and the sanctity of the earth in all its beauty."

He spoke for a long time and his words took on a rhythm like the beating of drums and I felt my troubles lift from my body and rise like smoke from a fire. I looked around and saw that the others felt the same. Even the Lakota who wanted me to leave felt it. The hatred, anger and prejudice rose up and out of our bodies.

I realized he was performing a cleansing rite. We formed a bond that would grow stronger in the days ahead. Together we would form a united front against those who would divide the cause. I felt welcome. I belonged.

I danced the Ghost Dance and joined the circle of the ancestors. On that sacred ground there were no distinctions of color or race and I swore I would never again perceive myself as a white man. I am a human being. That is enough.

I believe in the unity of all peoples. I believe in the sanctity of mother earth. I believe in the brotherhood of all beings. I believe we are all sacred beings in the eyes of the

Great Spirit.

The Lakota have a saying: Mitakuye Oyasin.

It translates to: All My Relations.

This is the message our brother the hawk brought to our gathering. This is the message of Black Crow. It is a vision of a new age and the center of a new circle of Ghost Dancers.

May it come to pass.

I will always remember the great Kiowa Apache spirit guide and the last words he spoke to us: You hold the future in your hands and the hope of the earth mother in your hearts. Hold on to it. For it is more precious than life itself.

Mitakuye Oyasin.

REPENTANT WARRIOR

I was a troubled youth, a rebel and a troublemaker. My teachers said I was out of control. They worried about my upbringing and moral fiber. The truth is I was angry – angry at the whites for how treated my people, angry at the names they called us and angry at how they made me feel worthless and stupid.

I did not understand then what I understand now: They stole something from me that I did not even know I had. They took my pride and my culture.

When I graduated high school I joined the white man's army and went to Vietnam. I wanted to prove to all those people who put me down that I was brave and strong. I wanted to be proud and I wanted my people to be proud.

So I killed for my country. I nearly died for my country. They gave me a medal but when I got home I found that no one was proud of what I had done. My family was glad that I was alive but they were not proud and I was not proud of myself.

I read an article that compared what the US government was doing in Vietnam to what they did to native peoples. It seems Americans love to hate people who are different than they are. We considered the Japanese inhuman, then the Koreans and the Vietnamese. We called them "gooks" and pretended they were not human beings.

I wanted to be a hero. Instead, like the traitors who killed Sitting Bull and the Apache scouts who tracked down Geronimo, I became the enemy. I betrayed my own people. I killed my own brothers and sisters.

I became what my parents feared. I did drugs and drank alcohol. I became a thief. I did many things I am ashamed of but mostly I drank. I drank for the same reason every man drinks: To forget, to kill the pain, to the fill the empty place where my soul should be.

They say an Indian forgets easier than white people. I don't know if that's true. I only know that when I was drunk I forgot and when I was sober I remembered. So I stayed drunk all the time.

Then I met a man named Black Crow. My father asked him to help me but the old man said I would have to ask for myself. They found me in an alley in Anadarko. It was morning but already I was too drunk to stand. Flies buzzed around the outside of my head and inside it felt like a battlefield. Cannons beat against my skull like the pounding of war drums.

I did not want anyone's help until I looked into Black Crow's eyes. I saw that my pain was not mine alone. It belonged to all Apaches, living and dead, and to all native peoples everywhere. We all suffer from the same disease, a disease of the spirit, a wasting of the soul. It leaves us standing alone, cut off from our families, our culture and history.

I struggled to my feet and like a wooden Indian that has no tongue I reached into my pocket for the only thing I had to offer. I pulled out a soiled pack of Marlboros that contained a single broken cigarette. I could not make this offering and I had nothing else to give. But he opened his hand and I gave it to him. He broke off the filter and smoked. In the way of our people it meant he accepted my cry for help.

We went to his house where I bathed and ate with his family. He then led me into a room without furnishings. There were blankets, pillows and a large ashtray on the floor. Blankets covered the windows, walls and the door. He told me these blankets were sacred. They had symbols of the sun, the earth, the moon and the stars, the buffalo, the wolf, the eagle and the hawk. Healers of many tribes blessed them. He lit sage and cleansed my body with smoke. He released pollen in the four directions. He marked my right foot and forehead with the cross. Then he said a prayer in the old language. A calm came over my body and my spirit. It was a feeling of peace I had not felt in a very long time.

Then we smoked and talked. I told him what happened in Vietnam: the villages we torched, the men, women and children we killed, the people who died by my hand. I talked and he listened, nodding, filling the pipe, smoking and lighting sage. I broke down and cried like a child, like a small, helpless child. I had never told these things to anyone, not even my family.

Black Crow said a prayer that soothed me. Then he spoke to me of Sand Creek, Medicine Bow, Wounded Knee and Indian Island. He spoke of the unspeakable crimes of the white eyes against the red-skinned people. I knew the stories but never before did I feel them. When Black Crow spoke I could hear the gunfire and the screams. I could smell the smoke and feel the wounds.

His message was not one of revenge. He spoke of the crimes our people had committed against the white eyes – settlers, hunters and others who only wanted to live on the land we shared. He spoke of the crimes of tribes against tribes so that I understood: None have clean hands.

He said we should not forget the wrongs of the past but right them by how we live today and tomorrow. In the end we are the sum of all that has been, all that is and all that will be. There is no reason to bow our heads in shame. There is every reason to rise and do right by our fellow beings.

Four days and four nights we talked, smoked, chanted and prayed. Together we walked the healing path. By the end of the fourth night I became a new man, reborn to the light of truth and wisdom in the knowledge of the old ways.

Since then I have never strayed. He healed my broken spirit. When a man heals your spirit he gives a part of himself to you and you become a part of him. We were bonded and he became the bridge that joined me to my family, my tribe and my people.

Years later when he asked me to join him in pilgrimage to Wounded Knee it was the proudest moment of my life. I looked upon his face when the young people joined in the Ghost Dance and felt the deepest warmth and love I will ever know.

Black Crow was the grandfather I never had. Today I carry his medicine bundle with pride.

GENTLE HEART

I am Whispering Willow of the Kiowa Apache. I am a healer, spirit guide, and wife to a great spirit healer who lies now in his final resting place.

My people know him as Black Crow. At one time they called him Walks Slowly and Crooked Leg. My own private name for him is Gentle Heart for he was the kindest and gentlest man I have ever known. We married young – so long ago I can no longer remember who I was before him. I see myself through his eyes and I believe he saw himself through mine. In the eyes of the Great Spirit and all that is sacred, we are one.

We married in the spring of the white man's year 1891 when the cottonwoods were in bloom and robins came to my window every morning. The sky was so blue I thought I could fly.

I believe I loved him since we were children. We played together until we were old enough to think, then we talked until we were old enough to think of other things. Then we were no longer allowed to be together. We kissed once and I knew I would always love only him.

My parents did not approve of the boy with the crooked leg. They believed as many did that an evil spirit touched him. They did not know him. They were stubborn like old mules. They said I would forget him. They said I would find happiness with another man – a good man who could hunt and ride and protect his family.

They were happy when Black Crow was chosen to make pilgrimage to the camp of Wavoka. It was a very long and dangerous journey. They did not believe he would survive. Still it was a great honor and I was proud. Many of the other young men were jealous. We held a big Pow Wow in his honor and the man who had taught and guided him gave him his name.

The old one's name was Coyote Eyes. He and the elders came to my home and told my parents it would give Black Crow strength and courage if he was promised the hand of their daughter. He said it would bring good fortune to our family. It was an honor they could not refuse.

They still feared Black Crow but they feared angering the elders more. They did not wish Black Crow harm but he was young. He had never joined a raiding party, never counted coup and never traveled beyond the small circle of our camp in Indian Territory. How then could he survive a journey of many miles through lands unknown to him, lands known to have many outlaws, killers and renegades?

Some felt the elders were offering him for sacrifice but Coyote Eyes took me aside to assure me that powerful spirits would guide and protect him.

"He is strong – stronger than anyone knows and he will be stronger still when he returns. He is a good man and he will become a great man."

I believed him. He said that the coyote spirit told him Black Crow would become a healer of the soul. He said that I was destined to be by his side.

When the first snows came and Black Crow had not returned I worried. When we heard about the massacre at Wounded Knee my heart sank. If the blue coats could kill women and children for dancing, what would they do to a pilgrim who could not run?

It was the longest winter I would ever live through. Each day I walked into the hills to a quiet place that was sacred to me. It was a place where I could feel the presence of the spirit world. I listened to the beating of my heart and the whistle of the northern winds. It soothed my soul. I built a fire and watched the smoke rise to the Overworld. I prayed to the ancestors and the Great Spirit to protect my love and guide him safely home.

I believe the Great Spirit heard my prayer for he spoke to me without words, healing my pain and comforting me. I knew Black Crow was alive.

When he finally rode into our camp I cannot describe the joy I felt. It was the happiest moment I would ever know. It was as Coyote Eyes said: He left almost a boy and returned a man. He rode tall on his horse though his eyes were heavy and solemn. When he dismounted I almost expected his leg to be straight but it was not so.

He looked at me with warmth and love. We embraced and our love became known to all the tribe. As we walked together through the camp the people smiled with joy. Even my mother gave her blessings.

He was called to a counsel of elders. They spoke for a long time as people gathered outside to learn the message he brought to us. When they broke counsel the elders told the gathering that the prophet was not a spirit being but only a man. They said that the Ghost Dance was still a sacred thing but we should keep it only in our hearts. It was not the will of the Great Spirit that we should die for dancing.

We married soon after and shared a long life together. He became a powerful healer. I also knew many healing secrets passed down from my grandmother and we became partners in healing.

Our medicine was strong. Times were hard for all Indian people and we were called upon to settle arguments, to comfort the grieving, to cast out evil spirits, to heal the sick and broken. We guided many lost souls back to the red road. We made many friends from many tribes and our family was never wanting.

We had a son and a daughter. We watched them grow into fine strong adults. Both went away to the white man's universities but they remember the old ways. Our son studied the medicines that heal the body and our daughter studied the medicines that heal the soul. They returned to the people and brought the old ways together with the new.

When Black Crow returned from his pilgrimage to Wounded Knee in 1975 he knew he would not live much longer. Now he lies on his deathbed and people of many tribes – Lakota, Paiute, Shoshone, Cheyenne, Kiowa, Arapaho and Apache – come to pay their respects.

My heart is both heavy and light.

There is no fear in his eyes. He speaks of a path of light he first saw at Apache Pass on his pilgrimage to Wavoka's camp. He knows he will soon walk that path to the Overworld of our ancestors. He promises he will wait for me and I believe him for in all these years he has never lied.

The people know him as a great healer and a man of the spirit but I will remember him for his gentle heart. His love for all people and all beings upon the earth is his legacy.

I ask the people not to mourn his passing. I tell them he has seen the path he will walk and the world in which he will live. I assure them it is a far better place even than this our beloved mother earth.

I ask the people to remember his words, his teachings and who he was not by the tribute of praise but by the tribute of living as he lived. For in the end there is nothing more a man may desire than that the world is better for his being.

May it be so.

APACHE PILGRIM

I. The Ghost Dance Apostles.

I am Kiowa Apache. I was born near Anadarko in present day Oklahoma. My brothers and sisters are the Kiowa and the Comanche of the southern plains but my blood, my culture and my language is Apache.

The elders tell how our tribe became separated from the rest of the Apache nation but that would take me far from my story.

Mine was the first generation of Apache to have no man, no woman and no child born in freedom. Even those who hid in the Chiricahua and Dragoon Mountains were not free as our parents and grandparents were to roam from the Black Hills of Wyoming to the Sierra Madres of Mexico. My tribe was confined to Indian Territory.

It was a great honor to be chosen to represent my tribe on pilgrimage to the camp of Wavoka, founder of the Ghost Dance. My journey would take me on an ancient trail of the Apache people and further west than any of my tribe had gone before.

It was the summer of 1890 when three men came from the northwest to bring word of the Ghost Dance. They were followers of Wavoka and carried a promise to spread his word and teach the dance to all tribes.

We had heard of the Ghost Dance – more from fearful white eyes than our Indian brothers. Wavoka prophesied that the dead would return to this world of the living. Those who believed in the old ways would prosper while those who did not would perish. Little wonder it frightened the white eyes. They pretend not to be superstitious but their religion is founded on superstition. The blue coats become dangerous when their people are frightened. Any provocation will set them to killing Indians. They believed the Ghost Dance was a war dance. They were wrong. It is a dance to give hope to native people but they believed what they believed.

The elders of the Kiowa Apache decided not to embrace the Ghost Dance with their whole hearts. They would only dance in secret, far from prying eyes, until one of their own had spoken in person to the prophet. They chose me to make pilgrimage. Why? Partly because I was not a whole man. I was born with a deformity. My left foot turns inward. I cannot run like the others. An Apache who cannot run is not an Apache – or so they said. I could ride a pony with the best but I could not run. When the Ghost Dance came to us I found I could do its shuffling side steps in a great circle as well as anyone.

Despite my deformity my people treated me with respect. For on the day of my birth, a great man of the spirit world had a vision: He said that I would become a great healer and guide in the hard times to come. He said I would have many powers but the greatest would be the power to heal a broken soul.

That is why the elders chose me. I was young and strong. I had attended the white eyes' schools and could speak their tongue. I could speak the Mexican tongue and knew words of other tribes as well. I knew the language of the hands and signals. I knew the ways of the ancestors and I learned much of our Apache brethren to the west. The elders instructed me to seek them out to join my pilgrimage.

I had a sound horse, a supply of venison, a Winchester rifle, a hunting knife, two pouches of good Indian tobacco, a sacred pipe and official papers from the Indian agency granting permission for my travel. We told them it was a mission of peace. Without their permission, the soldiers would kill or capture me and return me to the reservation.

I took special care of the sacred pipe, wrapping it thrice with deerskin, for if all went well I would present it to the prophet Wavoka.

I wore a white man's clothing – blue jeans, brown shirt and a round black hat – except for my moccasins. My people all dress like the white man now unless there is a Pow Wow or sacred ceremony. To wear Apache clothing would invite danger.

The elders gave me the path I would follow and told me where I would find Chiricahua, Mescalero, Lipon, Navaho, Comanche, Arapaho, Cheyenne and Paiute camps. They instructed me not to stray from the path until I reached the camp of the prophet.

My journey would take me across the Red River, the Pecos and the Rio Grande. I would cross the Mexico border into Chihuahua and travel north to the Chiricahua Mountains. I would visit my Apache brethren in San Carlos and Warm Springs. I would then go northeast to the western side of the Rio Grande and follow the river north to Denver, Colorado, where I would catch the Iron Horse to the camp of Wavoka.

On the day before my departure the tribe held a Pow Wow so I could bid farewell to my brothers and sisters, my fathers and grandfathers, my mothers and grandmothers. We knew it would be a long and dangerous journey. We knew I might not return.

There was a woman I had long desired and I was invited into the home of her mother. I was promised her hand in marriage when I came home. I don't think they expected me to return but I was grateful.

It was the moon of gaining power when I arose in the early morning and began my journey. If all went well I would reach the prophet's camp in two moons. If all went well I would return before the moon of the first snow.

II. A Kindred Spirit.

The first day I found my pace, an agreement between my spirit and the spirit of my horse, Fire Jumper. She was a strong red mare – not the fastest but durable – and our spirits joined well.

We forded the Red River before sunset. We made camp at a bend in the river where the cottonwoods grow and where the crow welcomed us with his caw.

We were joined by a strange white man traveling from the north. He scouted us before we spotted him. When he felt it was safe, he approached us, allowing us to inspect him before we decided to welcome him. He dressed in black except for his white shirt with a silver buffalo skull necklace. His hat was round and flat on the top like those worn by some lawmen and gamblers. He carried two pistols, a rifle and a hunting knife. I could see by the sag in his shoulders and the dust on his clothes that he had been traveling for many days. Still, there was dignity in his eyes and we had no difficulty inviting him to our camp.

He saw to his horse before sitting by the fire. He accepted my offering of jerky and offered coffee that I accepted in exchange. Then he told the story of his journey. He had traveled the west "from Dodge City to the Frisco Bay, from the Black Hills to old Chihuahua" for some thirteen years.

"I've rubbed elbows with every kind of renegade and chiseler know to man and lived to tell about it. I've smoke with Sitting Bull, gone face to face with Crazy Horse, and sat down a spell with the great Geronimo. I'm a dying breed and I've come to believe that the Indian is the noblest of all human beings. The name is William Faraday and I'm proud to meet you."

We shook hands and he looked at me as if expecting me to follow his lead. But a man on pilgrimage does not speak of his journey with strangers. Out of respect for his gift of tongue, I gave him one word: Pilgrimage.

He nodded as if he understood but his brow grew deep lines of thought and his eyes seemed to search mine for the answer to the mystery I presented.

"Wouldn't have anything to do with that feller, Jack Wilson, would it?"

Jack Wilson is the name the white man gave Wavoka. He sensed that he might be on the right track.

"You a Ghost Dancer?"

"What do you know about the Ghost Dance?"

Sensing that he solved the riddle, he said he knew the Ghost Dance had spread across the plains, everywhere where Indians lived and gathered, and wherever they danced the Indian agents sent for more soldiers.

"It's a disaster waiting to happen. I don't take sides, mind you, a man's got a right to dance but I will tell you ain't nothing good going to come of it."

I gave his words thought. I believed they came from a good place. He wanted to warn me.

"Wavoka says the ancestors will return."

"My friend, you go to Apache Pass in them Chiricahua Mountains and you will talk to your ancestors every night just about this time. Don't take a prophet to tell you that."

He looked at me with a twinkle in his eyes and asked, "That where you're headed?"

I nodded and we had to laugh. There was truth to his words and they knocked me off balance. I saw things in a different way. I liked this Faraday. He knew by my moccasins I was Apache and figured out where I was going.

"Thought we might ride together, friend."

"I would be honored," I replied.

It made the trail easier, the miles covered shorter, and if we encountered trouble his skill with guns would be useful. I told him about the life I left behind and what I would return to after my pilgrimage. I told him about the land grab the white man refers to as the Oklahoma Land Rush. They were in a hurry to steal what land remained to us. They not only stole our land but our identity as a tribe, taking tribal lands and allotting small portions to individual Indians. They made us live as the white man lives. We had to put up fences and live apart from our neighbors.

He listened to my story and nodded with sad eyes: "It's only the beginning, my friend."

He told me about the law the white fathers passed in Washington and how it applied to all tribes. I did not understand how a paper signed in Washington could take our land but so it was. I respected Faraday for telling me the truth no matter how much it troubled me.

III. Horse Thieves on The Pecos.

We rode for nine days, rising at dawn and keeping a good pace until sunset when we made camp. We made sure our horses were rested and strong. During the ride we kept mostly to ourselves, watching the land change as we approached the Pecos and then the Rio Grande.

The open skies and vast space of the Texas landscape gave me a feeling of freedom like the eagle yet alone like the coyote. There were times I wanted to ride forever, never returning to Indian Territory. At other times I felt so alone I wanted to turn back and go home.

At night we talked. I spoke of my people and our beliefs, our traditions and culture. I spoke of the agents and Indian School, my family and friends. Mostly I remained silent and listened to his tales of the Wild West. There were gamblers and gunslingers, whiskey and women. Sometimes he told stories about Indians.

He was a young boy in Denver when Colonel Chivington returned from the Sand Creek Massacre. He recalled how the soldiers carried scalps, ears, noses, fingers and the private parts of the men, women and children they killed. The town gave them a hero's welcome. It would be many years before he learned the truth: That Chivington attacked a sleeping camp of Cheyenne under a white flag of peace.

Faraday did not hide from the fact that he killed more than a few Indians but he never killed for sport. He killed only to protect himself and his companions. He talked about white traders giving Indians cheap whiskey so they could steal furs, buffalo hides and horses. He told me about gamblers cheating Indians out of their allotments.

I knew he told me these things to warn me and protect me from the temptations I would encounter on the road ahead.

"Never gamble with a white man," he said. "They've got more ways to cheat a man than an Indian has got uses for a dead buffalo."

"Never drink the white man's firewater," he said. "It's a vile mixture that'll make a man blind or strike him dead."

Most of his stories made me laugh but they always made me think.

Nights on the trail were dangerous. In the day we could see travelers far in advance and avoided those we did not wish to encounter. At night a campfire attracts all kinds of men, good and bad. Some men will steal anything they can and think nothing of killing for it. Those who have traveled know: The night traveler is either running from something he has done or planning to do something from which he must run. One of us kept watch while the other slept. If anyone approached we took cover until they passed.

Once when we were camped on the Pecos, a party of five men – two Mexicans, two whites and one Apache – approached our camp late at night. We took cover on opposite sides and watched them draw their guns, drinking whiskey, laughing and cursing in three languages. They trailed two horses and intended to add ours to their string.

One of the Mexicans said something about cowards hiding in the dark. He stooped to help himself to our coffee when a shot rang out, knocking his sombrero from his head. I let out a war cry and they answered with a half dozen shots into the night. Then my friend spoke in his deep and powerful voice:

"The name's Faraday! I've kilt more than you and a hell of a lot better, too! Drop those guns or I'll drop 'em for you!"

One after another they did as they were told until one of the white men decided to take his best shot. It was not a good one. Faraday shot him in the shoulder and it knocked him to the ground. The rest of them just stood there with their hands in the air.

We bound his wound the best we could and tied the lot of them up, hands to legs. They spit and cursed up a storm – all but the Apache who fell silent. His eyes filled with shame and I told him in my native tongue I would speak to the ancestors about him. I would ask for his forgiveness. I believe he understood.

Faraday took a piece of coal from the fire and wrote on a piece of white cloth: Horse Thieves. He tied it to a stick and planted it in the ground. We left them there. Depending on who found them, they would likely be hanged or murdered. It was not our concern.

As we rode on we realized we might not have survived the journey alone. When we came to the base of the Chiricahua Mountains, we shook hands as brothers and friends. With a heavy heart I thanked him for the company.

He turned west toward a small gambling town called Tombstone. I went north into the mountains. I wanted to reach Apache Pass before nightfall.

IV. Vision at Apache Pass.

The sun fell from the sky and the wind began its night song, sweeping through the canyons of the sacred mountains where Cochise was buried on his path to the Overworld, when I arrived at the pass. I saw a hawk circling in the distance and heard its call so I went to that spot, a small clearing in the rocky mountains. I sent up camp, lit a fire and burned sage to cleanse my body.

I drew a circle in the earth and carefully unwrapped the sacred pipe. I cast tobacco in the seven directions, said a prayer to the Great Spirit and sat down to smoke. In the way of my people every cloud of smoke is itself a prayer. I began to chant in words that did not belong to me or my tongue or any language that I knew.

A crow came to my fire and gazed into my eyes. I saw a land rich with tall trees, green grass, wildflowers, deer, wolves and bountiful herds of buffalo. Eagles circled in a clear sky. The mountains were filled with life. It was a land of infinite beauty as our mother intended. Then venomous clouds of smoke flowed from large metal pipes, poison poured into rivers, plants and animals died, leaving nothing but a barren land and smoke filled skies where all this beauty had been.

I saw a great circle of Ghost Dancers, chanting and praying, surrounded by blue coats with many guns, some with long strings of bullets larger than I had ever seen. The guns fired at once and hundreds of men, women and children lay dead. I saw snow cover the earth, freezing dead bodies in strange postures as if they still danced though their bodies no longer lived.

The crow fluttered away and four warriors on horseback came over the mountains from the four directions. I knew them as the great Apache war chiefs: Juan Jose Compa from the south, Mangas Colorado from the east, Victorio from the north and Cochise from the west.

They gathered around my camp and I was struck with a sense of calm, as if everything was as it should be, as if all would be well. They circled me on their mounts four times and were transformed into beings of light. The light surrounded me and entered my soul.

The light formed a path from where I sat to the western sky and there I saw a beautiful land full of life and wonder, all built of the same strange light. The warriors rode away on the path of light until they faded from my view. As I rose to follow the vision no longer appeared.

I awoke in the morning light, shaken and confused, yet I was filled with hope. I chanted and prayed for greater understanding. Why was this vision given me? What did it mean? Did it confirm or deny Wavoka's vision? A voice within answered that all would be revealed in time. It was the purpose of my journey and it would not be right to know the answers before I reached my destiny.

V. Broken Spirits.

On the ride to San Carlos, a reservation on the Gila River in Arizona, I replayed the vision in my mind, over and over, not trying to understand but seeing with new eyes, unclouded with thought or judgment. I finally let go and fixed my mind on the path ahead.

San Carlos is a miserable place, the pit of the earth, a place where only snakes and scorpions thrive, where nothing useful grows, where the wind fills the lungs with sand. It is a place designed to break the spirit. No one remembers the ancient wrong that brought the curse of mother earth but that is why the white man brought Geronimo here. They wanted to break his spirit. But Geronimo would not remain here. He and his followers fled from San Carlos again and again until they put him on a train and sent him across the land to the swamps of Florida where there was no place to run.

When I arrived there were many Apaches still here, scratching the dry land and living on the agent's rations. Their shoulders and heads bowed so that I could not see their eyes, I knew they no longer carried the Apache spirit within. They had become a different people.

The soldiers in charge refused to let me speak to the people. They were afraid I might undo what they had done. They feared that I carried Geronimo's fire. But there was little cause for fear. Not even Geronimo could reach their lost souls. I would pray for them as I prayed for my lost Apache brother back on the Pecos.

This was the sorrow that fell on all tribes across the land. It was a time of despair when the people looked back on a life that no longer existed. It was a time to remember all those who died trying to save a dying way of life. For every one that survived we remembered nine who left for the other world.

It was much the same at Warm Springs. I did not ask permission to speak to the people. I waited for nightfall and walked into their camp. Those who would talk to me told me they had not heard of the Ghost Dance and they wanted no part of it. They accepted the great change in their lives. They believed the Great Spirit abandoned them and they would not turn back. They would not raise their hopes only to be crushed again.

I could not blame them.

They had little food and too few blankets but it is the Apache way to share what little one has with a brother on the trail – especially a pilgrim on a sacred journey. But the Apaches of Warm Springs did not offer and I did not ask. It is a lapse I never thought I would see. I would carry it in my heart throughout my life.

When I left their camp an old man approached. He was a spirit guide and spoke to me of the sorrow that had claimed his people.

"We have heard of the Ghost Dance," he said. "It is a good thing. It gives poor Indians a reason to live. It helps us survive. There is nothing else that matters now. We must survive and we must keep the old ways alive."

He offered a gift of jerky and I accepted. It is the way of the Apache. He gave me a medicine bundle in a leather pouch and I tied it to my necklace.

"It is good strong medicine. It will give you strength on your journey."

We embraced and my heart grew lighter. I realized that

the Apache spirit still lived in this old man even after all he had seen. It gave me hope.

VI. Shadow of The Rockies.

I rode north along the Rio Grande to Colorado, watching the land change from desert to forest and back again until I came to the Great Rocky Mountains. Words fail to describe its grandeur: Towers of stone reaching ever skyward, piercing the clouds and pointing the way to the Overworld. I imagined climbing to their peaks and stepping off into the camp of the ancestors.

I camped four nights in the shadow of the Rockies and each night I heard the song of the ancestors in the wind. I believe they blessed my journey, my pilgrimage and my cause. I began to believe in the Ghost Dance.

I reached Denver on the fifth day. Denver is a strange town with many people – soldiers, gamblers, miners, women of the night, men with long beards and longer rifles, beaver hats, tall boots and shiny guns. As I rode down Main Street, passing drunken gamblers and saloon ladies lifting their skirts, hearing music that sounded like popping corn in fire, some of them jeered and spat at me. They called me names like savage, redskin and baby killer. They hated Indians. On most of their shops they posted a sign: No Indians Allowed.

I came to where the town ended. There were tents, shacks, stables, corrals and blacksmith shops. This is where all the Indians, the Mexicans, the blacks and Chinamen lived.

I was told a man could leave his horse here for a fee and it would be cared for while I traveled by train to Wavoka's camp and back. So I approached the first stable when a man of the Crow tribe caught my arm and asked if I intended to leave my horse in Denver. I replied that I did and he advised me not to leave it in this man's care. He said the white man would sell my horse and offer a broken down nag in its place.

"He makes his living stealing Indian horses. If you report

it to the sheriff, he only laughs at you. Many Indians leave their horses here. When they return from the Paiute camp they have no horse for the journey home."

He directed me to a place further out that was run by a black man with honest eyes. He promised to take good care of Fire Jumper and I trusted him.

VII. Iron Horse.

At the train station I was directed to the last passenger car. Reserved for Indians, blacks, Mexicans and Chinese, there were maybe a dozen Indians from many tribes, all pilgrims on the last leg of their journey to the camp of the prophet. The man seated next to me was an Arapaho spirit guide. He spoke English. We introduced ourselves and sat in silence a spell. He then spoke in a whisper that only I could hear.

"He is just a man."

I did not know if he intended this comment for me or for himself or some spirit being only he could detect. I knew he spoke of Wavoka.

"When I began this journey I wanted to believe. I prayed and chanted for the truth. But I had a vision. I talked to Wavoka. He told me he is just a man. He gives the people what they need to survive these terrible times. But the white man will not leave us in peace and the ancestors will return only in our hearts."

His name was White Wolf and I knew he spoke the truth. His eyes held the knowledge and wisdom of the ages.

I asked: Why do you tell me this? He told me we were both men of spirit and we had both had visions. I did not know how he knew this but I nodded and told him what my vision revealed. He listened to my telling and then he spoke:

"I have seen the smoke filled skies and the city of death. It is a place to the north the whites call Butte, Montana. They dig for the metals the wasichu loves more than family, more than the land and more than the god they worship. The smoke never stops pouring its poison into the sky. When they are done killing and poisoning the land and air, when there are no more metals to be dug up, maybe then they will offer the land back to the Indian. I have heard the last buffalo has already gone to the Overworld."

He shook his head and reflected on the destruction he had witnessed.

"As for the Ghost Dance massacre I do not know. I don't believe such a thing has happened but I fear it is yet to come."

I asked what he thought of the Apache warriors on the path of light. He said: It disappears before you because it is closed to you. It is the path of the dead.

We shared many thoughts on the long ride over the Rockies and across the high plains. We observed the open land, as vast as the imagination, yet wondered how it was not enough for the white man. They must have it all.

We talked about the future. He believed the Indian could survive but it would not be by becoming like the white man and living in his world. He believed we must remain apart from the white society and cause no trouble. We had to give up raiding and war parties and gambling in the white man's towns. We had to give up drinking firewater. If we caused no trouble and did not threaten the whites, he believed they would leave us alone, free to worship as we will, to believe what we believe, even to live as the ancestors did.

White Wolf was a very wise man. We walked together to the prophet Wavoka's camp.

VIII. The Prophet.

We came to a large clearing in a forest of pine and birch where hundreds of pilgrims from many tribes – Cheyenne, Arapaho, Crow, Blackfoot, Lakota, Ute, Navaho, Comanche, Kiowa, Ojibwa and more – gathered to see and hear the

118

prophet speak. It was the largest gathering of native people I had ever seen. We were welcomed, given food and blankets. They opened their hearts to us and we did the same.

We stood in a long line that led to Wavoka's wickiup, a large round shelter covered with birch bark, pine boughs and brush. When our turn came we entered and took our seats in a great circle. The prophet sat to the north. His translators sat beside him for those who did not speak English.

Wavoka spoke of being very ill for four days. In his fevered state he visited the ancestors and sat in counsel with the Great Spirit. He received a vision of how the wind and the earth would swallow the blue coat soldiers and how the buffalo would return to the world of the living. He received the chants and steps of a sacred dance that would bring his vision into being. He said that we should cause no trouble, that we should show no ill will toward the whites but that we should treat them as we would be treated. He asked us to go forth and spread the word of Wavoka.

In leaving we filed past the prophet one by one. Each of us gave him the gift we had brought from our tribes and he gave us his blessing in return. It was not easy to read this man. His eyes held wisdom but there was something else hiding in darkness like a truth withheld. I wondered if that darkness went by the name of Jack Wilson, the name the whites gave him.

We were not surprised by his words. What he said was what we had been told. White Wolf went off to be alone and seek the guidance of the Great Spirit. I understood but I was sorry to see him go. I would not see him again.

I stayed in Wavoka's camp three days and wished I could stay longer. The people there carried hope, not the kind of hope we shared at home, the kind that hopes we will survive the winter or the next great sickness but the hope that we will survive as a people with our own culture, our own traditions and beliefs. Seeing this hope in so many of our people, I thought once again: The Ghost Dance is a good thing.

But each night the sun fell earlier from the sky and I knew it was time to go. It would not be long before the moon of the first snow.

IX. The Long Winter.

I befriended a man of the northern Cheyenne. His name was Spotted Owl. Like myself, he was a young man who was chosen by his tribe to make pilgrimage. Together we rode the train back to Denver but when we got there we found we had no horses. The white man the Crow warned me about stole his. Mine was lost when the black man's stables and home were burned. It was the white man's doing but few would speak of it and nothing would be done. He took what remained of his belongings and left for Oregon.

Despite our own misfortune my heart went out to this honest man whose people were hated almost as much as the red man was. I prayed he would find peace in his new home.

Spotted Owl asked me to stay with his people in the north and I accepted. I don't know what would have become of me if not for his generosity. On foot I could not have made it home before the harsh snows of winter. As it was, with my crooked leg, the walk to his camp took three days.

His people took me in. They listened with rapt attention as we spoke of the spirit that surrounded Wavoka's camp. We agreed that the Ghost Dance was good but I told them as well of my vision and the words of White Wolf. We would be wise to take great care.

The snows came and we settled in. Food was in short supply and I fasted often. It was a hard long winter and every night we huddled together by the fire and listened to the wind whistling in the dark.

One night a man from the Oglala tribe came riding into camp. He told us of a place called Wounded Knee. He told us Sitting Bull was dead. Big Foot was dead. Hundreds of Lakota men, women and children lie dead on the frozen earth, murdered by the soldiers. I could not speak, my heart in my throat, as he described the massacre just as I had seen it in my vision. When he was done, the people looked at me with great sorrow but said nothing. Nothing could be said to ease the pain. There were only prayers and mourning.

We survived the winter and in the spring they gave me a pony for the long ride home. It was an honor and one that I accepted with humility.

The ride home was without incident. I spoke to no one and no one spoke to me. It was as if a shroud of mourning surrounded me. People went out of their way to avoid me. It was as if I had some horrible disease.

I arrive home to find little had changed. More whites had settled on our land. There were new hardships and conflicts with the agency but things were much the same. My people were surprised to see me. Most thought I had died. They threw a big Pow Wow in my honor.

When I told the elders Wavoka was just a man I could see relief in their eyes. They had received news of Wounded Knee and abandoned the Ghost Dance. I told them I still believed the Ghost Dance was good and that we should hold it in our hearts. They nodded but they did not believe. We never spoke of the Ghost Dance again.

Many years later, as an old man with many memories, I made a second pilgrimage. I traveled not by horse or train but by automobile. I rode with young people and held counsel with people of many tribes. I saw much hardship but I also saw much good. A time of rebirth had come to the world, a time when the word of the elders was again valued, a time when many reclaimed their culture and identity, and a time when the people were proud of their skin.

My pilgrimage did not take me to the Paiute camp or the Cheyenne village where I was granted refuge so long ago. I traveled north to Butte, Montana, where the smokestacks still spewed their poisons into the air. But the grass and the trees and the four legs had returned to the land. The mother's power is great. The earth heals. Even the buffalo survives.

My pilgrimage took me to the place where the Ghost Dance ended and where it begins again: Wounded Knee. Hundreds gathered to remember. All races and all tribes were represented there.

They danced four nights and I saw it was good. I thought of William Faraday, White Wolf and Spotted Owl, the old man of Warm Springs and Wavoka, himself. I wondered if he knew: The spirit of the ancestors is alive and strong. The Ghost Dance survives.

It is a good time to walk the earth, to breathe the air and see what you will see, for now I know the truth: All that is good survives and all that is bad slowly fades away.

FINAL PASSAGE

I am Black Crow. I lie in the place where I will soon leave this good earth. I am in the house that I have lived for many cycles of the sun. My wife, who is called Whispering Willow for the gentle path she walks, who I have loved longer than I have walked the earth, and my two sons are at my side.

Whispering Willow is troubled. I see worry in the lines of her face. I see pools of darkness form around her eyes. I cannot give her comfort. She is wiser than I am. What I know she knows and more. She knows I have walked this path before for I have told her of my visions. She knows I have been to the Overworld and soon I will be welcome there. She knows it is a place of beauty far beyond the wonders of this earth. She knows she will join me when her time comes.

Still, the sorrow will not lift from her heart. She says it is a blessing and a comfort at this time of passing. I have lived long and seen many things that opened the eyes of my heart and mind. I now understand enough to know I understand very little. I ask the Great Spirit to let this passing bring no more pain and suffering than is needed.

There is enough pain and suffering in this world already. It has been our purpose to ease the suffering. I am comforted that my wife is strong and that we have raised our sons to be as strong as she is – as strong as the oak that shelters our home. If she must walk the path a little longer, to bear the suffering and ease the suffering of others, it is because she is strong.

My time has come. My brother the crow has settled outside my window. It is a sign. The crow is my guide to the Overworld.

Willow is aware of the crow's presence. Tears fill her eyes yet her strength remains. As I look deeper and deeper into the eyes of the crow, my vision returns to me. I hear chanting in many tongues. I see campfires and Ghost Dancers in a clearing. I see four warriors on their mounts as they ride over the sacred mountains from the four directions: Compa, Mangas, Victorio and Cochise.

I see a fifth warrior who springs from the clouds to join them. It is Geronimo, the fiercest Apache warrior who ever lived. From the earth we are joined by my mother and from within we are joined by my father.

It is as it should be.

We are spirit beings, beings of light, rising to walk the path of light to the Overworld. I see the sacred mountains, fields of wildflowers, trees that never fall, clear lakes, rivers and streams. I see skies free of the white man's poison. I see the hawk, the eagle and great herds of buffalo. All is as it should be.

I ride with the great warriors of my people. We turn back to gaze upon the earth. It is the last time I will see her with these eyes. Willow is crying. She cannot stop the tears. She feels a loss but the sorrow leaves her. She sees what I see and comes to me. We embrace and I feel her strength one last time on this earth. She knows I will wait for her.

She smiles and the darkness is gone, the shadow removed from our spirits. She returns to earth and I ascend to the other world above.

I am Black Crow of the Kiowa Apache. I have learned that all things that live and breathe and walk upon the earth are sacred. I have walked a path of healing. I have received blessings from the Great Spirit, Mother Earth and Father Sky. I am grateful.

I ask that you remember me as one who tried to live in

harmony with all beings, as one who healed, as one who loved and lived with love in his heart. I ask my brothers and sisters to continue the work, to heal the great sorrows that divide and destroy us. I ask you to remember that we are all one being, one spirit, united with all spirits upon the earth.

Take good care of your father and mother for then they will take care of you.

I have lived my life and it is good.

Mitakuye Oyasin. Let it be so.

Big Foot at Wounded Knee
Photo by George Trager January 1891

RED MOON, BLUE SKY

I walk through a forest of poplar, elm and magnolia. The trees are barren, the air crisp, and the ground thick with dead brush and leaves so I know it is late fall or winter. Though it is night there is no darkness so I know the moon is full.

I climb a hill and come to a clearing at the top. I look up and see the red moon, not the golden red harvest moon of the Midwest but a ball of blood red fire. I drop to my knees, stunned, breathless, and find I cannot move. My eyes train to the eastern horizon, a crest of rolling hills in silver shadow.

I wait for the dawn to see if the sun is blue. Until then, I think of nothing else. My mind is frozen, my body still, my eyes focused to the spot where I expect to see the sun rise.

There is a large burst of light, spreading outward, silhouetting the hills. At first glance, the light appears blue – only a tint, only a suggestion of color. But before the sun appears, at the moment I expect it, I awaken and I am afraid.

I have had this dream for seven nights. Each night the moment of sunrise is a fraction closer. I have had no other dream than this.

It has been many moons, in the words of my grandfather, since I was a boy growing up on the Rez in Arizona, many moons since my grandfather died and I left that world behind. My grandfather was not a man of many words but those he spoke remained with me and became part of my being. His light has guided me from that day to this.

Yet even my grandfather's light cannot help me through

this vision for it was neither his nor that of the Apache people. It came from the north, a visitor from the Lakota nation who warned us of the end of the world. He told us there were many signs: earthquakes, floods, tornados, hurricanes, hard winters, changes in migration, the white buffalo, and all of these have come to pass. But the strongest sign and the seed planted deepest in my mind is that of the red moon, blue sun. It appears only at the end, when there is no more time for change, too late to alter the path. When the blue sun follows the red moon, there is only time for prayer.

The visitor, a very old man on his last journey, said nothing about dreams. The vision he described was as real as the floods and earthquakes we observe on the evening news. And so I am left to wonder: Is it a sign that signals the end of the world or a sign meant only for me? When the blue sun appears, as I fear it must, will the sky fall, the earth tremble, the waters sweep over the land, or will I alone crumble into dust? And after the fall, what then? Shall I/we rise like the Phoenix or descend like dark matter into the infinite void never to be seen again? Shall I/we be reborn to build a new and better world or fade into the oblivion of lost memories like the smoke of the last flame?

I quit my job as a janitor at Tennessee State University, explaining that my mother was very sick. It was not true. My mother no longer walks this earth. But my grandfather taught me never to burn my bridges. You never know what might happen. The world may not end. The sky may not fall. But if it does, I want to be with my own people – even though they may not recognize me. I want to be where home is more than a house where I lay my head.

I am alone in the world. Like the coyote, I have no family. I belong to no community. The few friends I have I have left behind. If I fall, there is no one who will comfort me. If I die, no one will mourn my passing.

My parents died in a fiery accident when I was a small child, too young to understand that parents do not grow on trees. When they leave you, they do not return. My sister drowned in the same swimming hole all the kids swam in every day of the summer. They said it was an undertow. I came to believe it was not an undertow. There was a dark cloud over my family – some ancient sin, some unknown crime against the earth mother. The people turned their backs on us. When my grandfather died, there was no one left. I was just old enough to strike out on my own and I did not look back – until now.

How I ended up in the land of the Cherokee and Choctaw I do not fully understand. I suppose it was where I landed when I got tired of the road. There was a woman – a singer-songwriter who liked the idea of being with an Indian. The love (whatever love there was) lasted less than six months. The relationship lasted a year.

A friend told me, with my Indian blood, I could make more money going to school than working. He was right. But after two years of schooling, I decided I would rather work and make less money. The university gave me a steady job and I settled in to the routine.

That was how it was before the dream came. Life should be a daily celebration, a rebirth, but for me it had become a struggle. I looked neither forward nor backward and there was nothing I desired. I awoke every morning without anticipation, without the drive that makes a day's labor pass effortlessly, without the simple joy of living, without the sense that something unexpected might happen to revive my spirit and bring a smile to my face. I lay down every evening without a prayer.

I began to drink—a little at first, then a little more. I knew where it was leading but I could not bring myself to care.

When the vision first came, I had no fear. If the world came to an end, what would it matter? It was then that I felt the pull of the homeland. It was then that I heard the cry of my ancestors, the defining need of my people to survive. I fought back against the apathy that shrouded my life with a dark cloud. I fought back against my growing dependence on alcohol, a need that had become my only reason for climbing out of bed. I set my house in order and, then, I set out for home.

Now, as I drive the last stretch of highway in an old Ford Galaxy, as I admire the haunting Gila Mountains on my way to San Carlos – a place where, Geronimo said, snakes and scorpions thrive while everything else withers and dies – I am having second thoughts. My gut is wound tight as the hide on an Indian drum. Afraid to sleep, afraid that the blue sun will appear before I have reached my destiny, I am so full of caffeine I can feel the lids scrape against my eyes when I blink. I am tired, unbalanced, cranky, and the sun is falling like a stone in the western sky.

I am afraid to go on, afraid to turn back, and all the reasons I left the reservation come back to me like a torrent of rain: Alcoholism, drugs, poverty, welfare, wasted lives and broken spirits. The young turned their backs on the elders and the old ways were buried with the old. I am struck with the realization that I have become all that I wanted to leave behind. A man becomes what he most fears.

So now I am heading back to a place that no longer exists, that has not existed for a hundred years: The homeland of the Apache. I have lived so long in the white man's world I have almost forgotten what it is to be Apache. Like the snake, I shed my red skin and became a white man.

For a thousand miles, I have fought a powerful urge to pull into a trucker's bar and drink myself to distraction. Now, unable to keep my eyes on the road, I pull over at a roadside café on the outskirts of San Carlos. I am thirty miles short of Bear Mountain – a sacred place, a place my grandfather went to seek a vision, and a place he brought me to learn the old ways. Only thirty miles from my destination but I cannot make it without another cup of coffee, without a breath of fresh air and a moment of peace.

APACHE JACK

I sit at the counter, flip over a coffee cup, and glance at the waitress, an attractive Apache woman with long, braided hair. She acknowledges me with her eyes and continues a conversation with two older men, both Apache. I let my eyes close for only a moment and suddenly *I am walking through a forest of elm and magnolia. The trees are barren and the air crisp, the dead leaves thick on the forest floor...*

"Hey, buddy!"

I awaken to a hand gently nudging my shoulder. I open my eyes and the waitress is smiling, pouring coffee.

"I don't mind you sleeping," she says, "but I'm afraid you might fall off the stool."

The two men are heading for the door. They stop and wait until she signals them with a nod, as if to say, "It's okay." They leave and the bell over the door jingles like wind chimes. Funny I did not hear it when I came in.

The waitress leans on the counter, watching me gulp down the coffee.

"Where you headed?"

"Bear Mountain."

She refills my coffee.

"You know your way around?"

"Yeah."

She pours herself a cup and sits two stools down. We are alone in the café.

"I used to know someone who looked a little like you," she says. "Only younger."

I begin to wonder at this conversation. She is much too attractive to be making a play at a stranger. I decide she must be bored.

"It was a long time ago when I was a little girl and he was in high school. He played shortstop on the baseball team."

My smile betrays me. My first stop in Indian country and already I am spotted. It was the last thing I expected.

"Billy Hawkeye?" she asks.

131

I nod. It is my Apache name, a name I have not used in ages. My driver's license now reads: William H. Smith. I try to place her but I cannot. She laughs. "Sarah Running Water," she says. "I don't expect you to remember me."

But I do remember her. Her brother was a rare friend and her family was one of the few my grandfather respected. They kept the old ways in their hearts, passed down in stories through the generations, even when all seemed lost. They cared for the less fortunate when crops failed, gardens withered, and handouts came up short.

Like my grandfather, I am a man of few words but Sarah Running Water's presence, like a shining light in dark skies, inspires and humbles me. She is ten years my younger but she has an acquired wisdom, an instinctive understanding beyond her years. I tell her my story from beginning to end. I tell her my dream, which I have shared with no one else.

She listens intently, commenting only when I pause to collect my thoughts or rub my failing eyes. When I have finished, a smile returns to her face. Her dark, penetrating eyes hold the light of stars.

"You have come home," she says.

Spoken aloud, the words strike me with the force of a thunderbolt. For the first time, I believe them. I have come home – not to a barren wasteland, nor to a place where I am neither known nor welcome, but to a place where a friend greets me with a warm smile and embraces me with kind understanding. I have answered the call of the ancestors and already I am rewarded.

She advises me not to fear my dream but to embrace it. She says it is wrong to fight the rising of the blue sun.

"Welcome it," she says, "as you are welcome."

I realize it is the advice my grandfather would have given. Her eyes enchant me and I recognize in them a familiarity, a similarity to my grandfather's eyes.

"You need sleep," she says. "There's a cot in the back.

Tonight the moon is full. We'll go to Bear Mountain together."

I don't question her. I trust her. I believe in her eyes. If she had advised me to go back to Tennessee, I believe I would have done so.

I walk through a forest of barren trees. As I begin to climb a small hill, I raise my eyes to see the red moon. Yet I am not afraid.

I reach a clearing at the top of the hill. I kneel to grab a handful of earth and make an offering to the spirits of the four winds, to father sky and mother earth.

I sit to wait for the dawn.

I am not alarmed to hear footsteps at my back. The hand on my shoulder is expected, her presence behind me, beside me, calming, comforting.

The moment of sunrise spreads light on the hills of the eastern horizon. Still I am not afraid.

Another hand on my shoulder...

"Time to go, Hawkeye."

I blink my eyes awake and feel a surge of energy from within. I am rested and clear. Sarah has changed into jeans, a blue work shirt, embroidered with the sun and moon, and hiking boots. I sit up, stretch, and she looks at me with her dark, knowing eyes, anticipating my words.

"The sun is blue," I tell her.

She nods as if she already knew and the disarming smile that first welcomed me returns to her face, as if to comfort me once again.

We ride to Bear Mountain in silence. I realize that, like an idiot, I have not asked about her life, about the path she has taken to this crossing. I am so absorbed in my own drama that I have forgotten the basic rules of communicating with a woman. I also realize that my spirit is too clouded to listen with my heart. It will wait.

The sky is clear and the moon is high and white as pure cotton, glowing like a florescent lamp. We pull off at an overlook and hike to a clearing, which I recognize as the place my grandfather brought me. We gather wood and build a small fire. We spread a blanket and it is Sarah who first makes offerings to the six directions. I follow her example. We sit to wait for the dawn. The view opens to the east and in the distance we see the tall peaks of the San Francisco, Gallo and Mongollan Mountains – nothing like the rolling hills of my dream. We speak very little but when we do it is mostly of the old ways, the old days, the things our elders told us. She confides that she, too, has struggled with the desire to break free of reservation life. She attended the University of Arizona but only for a semester. The pull of the family and the people was too strong. She chose to stay.

The night is cold and we huddle together under blankets for warmth. More than a few times we gaze into each other's eyes, seeing into each other's souls, and our spirits embrace. Huddled together in the desert moonlight, waiting for the sun, we become one with the land, one with the mountains, one with the nighthawk overhead, one with the flames before us, one with all we see and one with the old ones that still live within us.

I sense my grandfather's presence as the sunlight first appears on the distant peaks. The mountains are dark blue but the light is golden. The sun bursts through like a rising Phoenix and I am filled with wonder.

"White moon," says Sarah. "Yellow sun."

Our lips slowly and gently meet and I understand clearly what she has understood all along: The dream of the red moon, blue sun was mine and mine alone. I had come to a place in life when I needed death, for it is death that finally calls us home. My life ended when I left Tennessee and was reborn here on Bear Mountain. I was reborn to my people, to my ancestry, with the woman I hope will share my new life at my side.

APACHE JACK

My grandfather once said at a ceremonial funeral: From the ashes new flames will rise; and from the dust, new life. I give thanks and recall the last words of a great Lakota warrior: It is a good day to die.

THE KILLING SPIRIT

I. I had to get out.

I had to get out when every breath was her voice singing, when every step was her rhythm walking, when every song was Maria talking, driving, laughing, praying, crying, screaming, dying, when every mountain was the shape of her dance, the lines of her kiss, the form of her breast, the arch of her back, the curl of her hips, the taste of her love, her tongue in my ear, her tongue, her taste, her breath.

I had to get out before I became a dead woman's memory, before her ghost swallowed me whole and my spirit left me for a walking corpse.

I took to the road.

Crying for a Vision, Grandfather said. What the white man calls a Vision Quest. "When you have had your vision, you will come home."

I leaned my head out and took in the smell of cattle, the smell of hay, the smell of manure and horses, pigs and farms, the smell of crew cuts, cheerleaders, red wood barns and white picket fences. "Kansas," I smiled.

A sign: Saint Louis 234 miles.

Lala (for Lollapalooza) did a shimmy so I gave her some gas. She lurched and galloped down the open road, chasing the White Buffalo, seeking the Red Road on the Blue Highways, following my ancestors to the mountaintop where I would cry for a vision. I had been riding for three days and already I knew my pony better than in the twelve moons since she came to me.

The radio sputtered and I gave the dial a spin with a rap on the dash. A mourning wail of fiddles emerged. It was Neil Young and Crazy Horse. It was the white man with a red man's spirit. It was the man who overcame his white man advantages and learned to speak the tongue of the great Lakota war chief. And now Crazy Horse, who led his warriors into battle on a white Appaloosa, was delivering a message to his great, great grandson, Jerico Whitehorse.

I pulled over to the side of the road and let the dust settle. I turned off the engine and tuned my ear to the hum of cicada. I walked a slow circle from east to south to west to north, scanning the surroundings of scattered farm houses, patches of green grass, rows of corn, groves of maple and Kansas oak, looking for signs. On the third circle, a crow sounded to the east and flew to the south.

I knew what I must do. I would follow the path of the crow east to the waters of the great river and then south where the Lakota always faced, south to the beginning and the source, south where the winged one protects the sacred path, and south where all the generations emerge and where they return. There I would cry for a vision.

II. The waters of the great river.

I let the waters of the great river wash over me. Driving south along the eastern bank, I let go of my thoughts, my dreams, my ghosts and shadows. I let go the past as I watched the vines and brush of an eternal forest creep over the ruins of the white man monuments. I watched the power of the earth in motion, reclaiming the land from the discards of the white man's industry – rusting appliances, decaying vehicles, tin sheds and plastic waste. I felt the air grow heavy and alive with insect life as sweat covered my skin and great, sprawling trees, magnolia, oak and dogwood, threw shadows on the blue pavement.

A woman with flying red hair in a blue convertible passed me on the narrow road in a blur of rock and roll glory. A chill crawled up my spine as three doves crossed over the tree line to the west. Caw of a crow and silence.

I nudged Lala into a slow canter and wound down the road of shadows. I saw Marie, the woman I had loved and lost, in the mirror of my memory. He saw her smile turn to lifeless form. I saw her body dancing transformed to unformed clay. I saw her blood on the pavement of a lost highway. I saw her tears dry as mine raged.

I saw Marie behind and Marie ahead, as I rounded a curve where an old pickup had been forced off the road and the driver knelt coughing blood and bleeding from his forehead. I pulled off my shirt and pressed it to the man's head, guiding him away from the trail of spilled gas and the thick, dry brush, coaxing him to lie down on the side of the road.

"To hell with me!" the man cried through the blurred vision of his blinking eyes. "Help her!" He gestured to where the woman with red hair went over the edge. I saw a trail of burning rubber, a splintered guardrail, and a path of fresh destruction.

I skidded down a steep embankment and dove into the muddy waters as the overturned car went under. There was life in her eyes when I reached her but her struggle to survive was gone. Her body was still when I pulled her to the bank, still when I pushed the water from her lungs, and still when I tried to breathe life into her.

The woman was dead. Marie was dead. Nothing I did could save her or bring her back. I heard laughter, cruel laughter, in the river running, laughter in the wind through the tall trees, laughter in the wail of sirens and the whirl of red lights and firemen barking orders and rescuers shoving and police asking questions.

"What did you see?"

I saw a woman die. I saw her spirit leave this earth. I

saw Marie. I sat down in the shade of a magnolia and wiped the water from my eyes.

"It was an accident," someone said. "Nothing you could do." But I did not believe in accidents. It was a sign, a bad sign, an omen of death, and it left me with an empty, hollow, helpless feeling.

III. Something in the woods.

There was something in the woods, something dark and secret, like a wisp of cold air on the back of the neck or the grim stare of a stranger in a crowded room. A pallor hovered over dogwood and oak, like a demonic shadow, like a curse, like an invisible fog with a pounding, pulsating core, like the heart of darkness itself, an uncompromised evil, its thumping rhythm emanating in concentric circles, moving and growing like waves of sound imperceptible to the human ear, softened only by distance and time.

Dogs howled, owls took flight, and the forest dwellers fastened their windows and doors. There was something in the woods.

IV. The path of the Cherokee.

I left the great river behind. Turning east near Memphis, I followed the path the Cherokee walked in a century no longer remembered by the white man's history. The Cherokee remembered and I remembered with them. I pulled off the road and listened to the haunting night song of hoot owls, tree frogs, cicada and the nightingale. This was the Trail of Tears where the lost souls of the civilized tribe still walked the long summer nights.

On this night, I walked with them. I shared their sorrow, their suffering, their defiance and courage. I saw men carrying women, women carrying children, and the strong carrying the dead. I saw the clarity in their eyes, their faces wiped clean of expression. It was a march of destiny. They would reveal no pain, no fear, not even pride, though it marked their every step. They would give the whites no show for their misfortune, nothing they could hold in their hearts and minds for further hatred and vengeance. What was their crime but to perceive themselves as human beings, entitled to fundamental rights and human dignity? Even the children did not show fear. They marched blankly in an endless progression, eyes dead ahead, following the sun to where souls go to die.

I saw the tears of strangers alongside the trail – whites, blacks, working people – choked by their impotence and guilt for they had not suffered enough. They did not have the courage or the right to march with them. They did not belong to the land as the Cherokee did, as the Lakota, as the Cheyenne and Comanche did. I saw the march of generations, mothers and fathers, sons and daughters, grandmothers and grandfathers. I saw a child in the arms of her mother. I saw the ones that fell off the path and found their way back to their own land in the mountain forest of copperheads and red tails. I saw and understood: All my relations. Mitakuye Oyasin.

V. Land of the Mound Builders.

Following the path of the crow, I followed the Natchez Trace, a scenic highway that was once the artery of a native empire ruled by five tribes known as the Mound Builders. They were among the first to greet the invaders from across the great waters and to recognize what their arrival would mean to the native peoples.

Covered in the sweat of sweltering, liquid heat, I pulled off the highway looking for refuge. I found it in a workingman's bar with a blue neon sign: Ice Cold Beer.

Settling on a stool I ordered a cold one on tap over the quiet drone of country music. I watched the patrons in the mirror behind the bar take note of my braided hair, red bandana and native features, but I was surrounded by a faraway aura that shielded me from routine harassment. No one was eager to disturb the peace of a crazed Indian – not in this heat. They left me to my thoughts. I kept my eyes straight ahead and sipped my brew.

The dim lighting went dimmer and a whistling sound filled the room. I looked around. No one reacted. I heard the soft whisperings of a couple at the far corner of the bar in perfect clarity. I heard roaches scrambling beneath the sink, flies in the kitchen, water in pipes, the hum of 60-watt light bulbs, and beneath it all, I heard something like a voice.

I heard a humming, pounding sound – a thrumming. It came in waves and pulses, pounding and subsiding, and with the sound came pictures, random pictures, portraits of the damned, contorted faces like those in Dante's Inferno, young and innocent faces, faces marked with age and disease, wise faces, innocent faces, faces that had known sorrow and faces that knew only the warmth of love and family. The only distinction was that they were all Indian faces.

I heard screams of agony and crawled inside their skins so I could feel their helplessness and pain until it drew me from the barstool and pushed me like a madman out the door where I fell to the ground, gasping, choking, sweating cold.

Some of the patrons followed me out as the pounding, thrumming waves of sound receded into the woods. "I'm alright," I said. They watched and waited until they were sure I was not dying. Then they went back inside to make deriding comments about those "crazy fuckin' Indians."

VI. The killing spirit.

I steadied my hold upon the earth. I felt raped and abused and fear swelled in my pounding heart. I wanted to get out. I wanted to grab Lala's reins and ride into tomorrow but something stopped me. This was my enemy. This was the enemy of my people. I remembered my vow when I became a man and a Lakota warrior: You will not turn from your enemy. A warrior does not always choose to fight but when the battle is chosen, the warrior's life is his honor. It does not matter how strong the enemy is. The warrior plants his staff and makes his stand. Crazy Horse did not run from Custer and I would not run now.

I pulled out my hunting knife, rose to my feet and followed the thrumming into the woods. I found a trail and held to it, slicing through overgrowth, bristles, bushes and creeping vine as the thrumming, whistling, pounding sound intensified. I tried covering my ears but the sound was both within and without. I hiked until the sun fell from the midday sky, until the green of the forest turned dusk gray and slivers of light shot through the trees like lasers.

The sound softened and I slowed my pace. I was standing in a gorge, limestone bluffs pressing in on both sides. It was a place ripe for an ambush. I backtracked, climbing the northern bluff, and crept forward until I was perched above a clearing where the waters of an underground spring trickled through the limestone into a small pond surrounded by wildflowers.

I gazed down upon a beautiful girl of twelve or thirteen, dressed in white with beaded white buckskin moccasins and a matching vest, her long dark hair in a single braid, sitting Indian style on the rocks, teasing the water with a stick. I recognized the beadwork as Cherokee and sensed that she was dressed for ceremony. The Lakota call it: Making a Girl into a Woman.

I was careful not to disturb her but when the thrumming returned, when the skies darkened and a blanket of dark clouds moved overhead, I called out to her. I cried out again but she could not hear. She did not see what I saw. She did not sense danger, though the pounding sound was now so deafening it bent me to my knees.

I pressed my forehead to the ground and summoned my

strength but the pounding only grew stronger, shaking my bones, rattling in my skull, boiling my blood with fear and rage. I struggled to rise up, to curse this darkness, to challenge this evil hiding in shadows like a devious coward. What is this spirit that fears to show itself?

The pounding ceased, the clouds lifted and the darkness vanished almost as quickly as it appeared. The forest breathed again and so did I.

I looked down to the girl and froze to the place where I crouched. A man with hunched shoulder, a flash of metal, arms flailing, hitting, scratching, kicking, blood, screaming, moaning, a knife in her chest, her body writhing in a pool of red, eyes wide open, his face in her eyes, yet I could not move. The girl screamed and I could not move. I could only listen to the beat of her fading heart and the barbed laughter of the killing spirit.

I understood that the spirit had led me to this place, wanting me to witness this horror. The killer expected me but had he expected me to backtrack? If not, he would expect me to appear on the trail below, not on the bluff above where I now crouched, crippled by the darkness, paralyzed with fear. I prayed to the Great Spirit, to the ancient ones, to the Ghost Dancers at Wounded Knee and the ghost walkers on the Trail of Tears, to all who died at Sand Creek, Medicine Bow and Indian Island. I prayed to the spirit of the crow, the buffalo, the wolf, the Appaloosa and the great thunderbird. I called upon the spirits of Sitting Bull, Black Kettle and Big Foot, and all those who had suffered at the hands of the wasichu.

When I summoned the spirit of my great, great grandfather, I felt my body awaken from its slumber. I sprang from my perch and soared like the night owl silently to my prey. My grip sank like talons into the killer's shoulders, grasping him with viselike fear and breaking his will like a severed spine. The killer crumpled to the earth, a limp body of useless flesh.

I spun the killer around and, poised to strike with my hunting knife, challenged my enemy to confront the moment of his last breath in the eyes of the one who killed him. Gazing at this despicable being, my eyes were the eyes of all my people, living and dead: Red Cloud and Little Big Man, He Dog and Two Feathers, Young Man Afraid and Spotted Tail, Black Elk and No Water, Crazy Horse and Black Buffalo Woman, Geronimo and Red Sleeves, LaDuke and Peltier, Crow Dog and Lame Deer. In the moment of vengeance, I became all my people yet I could not strike the blow.

The glimmering blade of justice clung to the sky, freezing time to a crystalline moment. Sensing my struggle, the face of the killer revealed shame and cowardice, though his eyes reflected a thousand deadly faces: Long Hair and General Miles, the unnamed coward who plunged his bayonet into Crazy Horse as Little Big Man held his arms, the Colorado volunteers who cut from Cheyenne women their most private parts and fixed them to their saddle horns, the railroad men and their buffalo slaughters, the Appaloosa killers, the thunderbird killers, the river killers, the earth killers.

The killing spirit wore so many faces, an endless sea, wave after wave, as infinite as the stars, and each carried the darkness beneath his pale skin, each deathly afraid and filled with hate. Two thousand years of hatred and slaughter, two thousand years of white man dominance, yet still they fear and hate.

Perhaps they hate because they fear. Perhaps they fear because they know what they have done.

The man pleaded for a merciful end. "Kill me," he moaned. Like Custer's soldiers, who killed themselves before they could be killed by Lakota warriors, the killer begged for death.

I realized that this man was not my enemy. He was the hand of the killing spirit but he was not its heart. His was the small soul of a little man. The darkness that was the enemy of my people lived inside this man but it would survive his death. The real enemy was the fear, the hatred, the need to dominate and destroy those who stood opposed. Killing was all the wasichu had ever known.

I recalled the first time I was told of the white man's religion. *They have killed their own God*, I thought. Now they will kill everything in their path until their God returns to have his just revenge. They want to be tortured, beaten and whipped, as they have tortured their enemies. They want to be struck down and killed as they struck down and crucified their God. They lack the courage to take their own lives so they pray for their God to return and take them. But the white eye's God will not return. They have killed him. He is dead. So their anger has no end and their killing never stops.

I released the killer and watched him disappear into the forest. I heard a muffled cough and turned to the bloodied body beside me. She was alive. It seemed to me: As I had spared the wasichu killer, so the killing spirit spared her.

VII. The Girl Who Became a Woman would live.

She was badly wounded, bleeding and mercifully unconscious but I knew she would live. She had earned her womanhood in a struggle for life. She had fought as a cornered wolf with all her strength and courage. As she became a woman, I reflected, so I became a man. We had made a stand against millennia of suffering and struggle. We planted the staff together, Lakota and Cherokee, and faced the enemy.

I remembered Crazy Horse's vision of death, his hands held by his own people. Crazy Horse had seven visions in his life. Now I had my first. It was a vision in flesh and blood and one that would guide forever my path on the red road. It was a vision of justice and sacrifice, honor and courage, vengeance and mercy. I knew in my heart how it must end.

I thanked the Great Spirit, the four winds, the six directions and all my relations. I asked the blessings of my great, great grandfather: The Girl Who Became a Woman would live.

I bound her wounds, cradled her life in my arms and carried her out of the woods.

ABOUT THE AUTHOR

Jack Random has lived at once an ordinary and extraordinary life. His roots firmly planted in the fertile central valley of California, he has marched the streets in protest, haunted jazz town bars, read poetry in cafes and town squares, strutted his hour upon the stage, crisscrossed the country by air, rail, highway and thumb, mourned at Wounded Knee, gazed into the eyes of the crow at Grand Canyon, and paid tribute at the grave of Geronimo. He has labored in the fields of plenty, toiled on the assembly line, pursued higher education and attempted to enlighten children in the public schools. He has been a pilgrim and a seeker of truth. He is married to the love of his life. All the while he has chronicled his thoughts and revelations in words: plays, poetry, novels, stories and essays. His first novel *Ghost Dance Insurrection* (Jazzman Series) was originally published by Dry Bones Press (2000).

OTHER BOOKS FROM CROW DOG PRESS

Wasichu: The Killing Spirit – A Novel by Jack Random. A modern day telling of the life of Crazy Horse recalls the history of Native America and its most revered leader.

Number Nine: The Adventures of Jake Jones and Ruby Daulton – A Novel by Jack Random. A woman on the run picks up a hitchhiker and takes us on an adventure that winds its way to New Orleans in the summer of Katrina.

A Patriot Dirge – A Novel by Jack Random. Political genius Roman Mason takes on the political and economic forces that rule our lives (Jazzman Series).

Jazzman Chronicles: Volumes I–X – Essays by Jack Random. Political commentaries from 2000 to 2014.

A Mother's Story – Stories, Art and Reflections by Artis Brown Miller. A mother of eight children reflects on a life of hardship and love.

Pawns to Players: The Stairway Scandal – A Novel by Jack Random. An aristocrat and a billionaire play a chess match to determine the fate of the American government.

The Grand Canyon Zen Golf Tour – A Memoir by Jack Random. Two friends embark on a journey of golf, music, poetry and family in the summer of 1993.

Hard Times: The Wrath of an Angry God – A Novel by Jack Random. Not with a bang but a whimper the end of days comes.

Pawns to Players: A Match for the White House – A Novel by Jack Random. Part two of the Chess Series.